LINES OF
LIGHT

Daniele Del Giudice

LINES OF LIGHT

Translated by Norman MacAfee
and Luigi Fontanella

A HELEN AND KURT WOLFF BOOK

HARCOURT BRACE JOVANOVICH, PUBLISHERS

San Diego   New York   London

Library of Congress Cataloging-in-Publication Data

Del Giudice, Daniele.

[Atlante occidentale. English]

Lines of light / Daniele Del Giudice ; translated by
Norman MacAfee and Luigi Fontanella.

p. cm.

Translation of: Atlante occidentale.

"A Helen and Kurt Wolff book."

ISBN 0-15-152420-3

I. Title.

PQ4864.E4377A913 1988

853'.914—dc19

87-35910

Designed by Camilla Filancia

Printed in the United States of America

First edition

A B C D E

To Silvia

I

On the runway he tested the rudder, then opened the throttle and started to roll. The yoke pressed his elbows into his ribs, and the plane's tail, trailing, pushed his head forward, which split his field of vision between the dials on the instrument panel and the trees in the distance, as if he were wearing bifocals. The course before him was in reality an adjustment to everything inside and outside the airplane, including his face elongated in the sun and the curving Plexiglas.

Every airfield, an area more open than the city it borders, has a pastel hue that gives solidity to things; it also contains a point of convergence where velocity coincides with sound. As he sped toward that point, the hangar, the fuel pumps, and the renting office fell away beneath him. He would be able to feel the exact moment, but kept his eye on the tachometer until he lifted off.

There was a flash to the right, in the trees, bearing down on him, another plane flying at an angle, so close and low that his cockpit would be hit by the propeller. He veered, pushing the stick forward and killing the engine. A long white belly passed over him roaring, sweeping, intimate, like a slap in the face.

He was on the ground once again, the plane skidding. He avoided sudden maneuvering, but gently resisted as he submitted to each change of direction, until he slowed and equilibrium returned. At the edge of the field, he turned and came to rest. Head close to the Plexiglas, he searched the sky for the other plane: checking calmly, as if nothing had happened.

On the runway again, he taxied toward the hangar. The low morning sun, facing him, was encircled by the shadow of the turning propeller. Accelerating, he could raise the rear tire and, decelerating, lower it instantly. Like being in a car, except that on the ground the wings cause drag, and the seat is uncomfortable. It seemed the airstrip would never end.

He parked on the concrete pad, locked everything, and climbed out. The mechanic raised his head from an engine he was repairing and said, "All finished, Monsieur Brahe?" He spoke the stiff French all Swiss speak.

"I didn't even start," the young man replied.

The mechanic got down the stepladder, wiping his hands. He approached Brahe, who had crouched near the landing gear. The young man was moving his hand on the fork as on an animal's hoof: checking its alignment. "Problems?" the mechanic asked, bending down beside him.

"I had a near miss." He fingered the metal, looking for a scratch or dent: "Who flies a white Zlin?"

The man in overalls turned toward the hangar, toward the airplanes lined up in the semidarkness, and focused on the empty spot: "It's not rented. It's a private plane. It must be someone who comes to fly very early in the morning."

"Earlier than me?"

"Yes." The mechanic smiled. "Very early. When I get here, the plane is already back, covered with a tarpaulin. You can tell he flew only because the grease spots are not in the same place on the cement. It doesn't get moved often. It is strange he has not returned yet."

Brahe straightened, hands in his pockets, listening to the mechanic, still looking at the plane. "I don't think there was any damage, but we better check." He was too tense for explanations, and he was beginning to feel a sharp pain in his ribs, where the seat belt had held him in. The mechanic placed both hands on the wing and pushed down, leaning over sideways to look at the landing gear. It was indeed his job, he said, to test the landing gear again, and he would do that as soon as he returned from Geneva, where he was going to get some parts. Unbuttoning his coveralls, which dropped to the ground in a heap around the gray trousers he was wearing, he told Brahe that Brahe might not be refunded all his money but would be reimbursed, at least, for the unused fuel. Then he got into a yellow van with a sliding door, said good-by, and left.

It was only then that the Zlin reappeared over the airfield, in wide, slow circles, making a monotonous hum, so slow that it seemed immobile. It seemed that it was the earth that circled and rose to meet it, but Brahe could not tell whether the center of that rotation was somewhere in the field or in himself. He walked to the runway and, with his arms folded, stopped on the mown grass, between two parallel rows of unlit lights set into the ground. He watched the plane. The pilot must have seen him, as he must have seen him before.

To Ira Epstein the future was observation from a height: a diverse symmetry of greens and grays composed mostly of fields, woods, and an occasional visible structure. It was the ability to become small, potent, and indistinguishable from these artificial patterns. It was a vertical jut of aluminum or cement, now and then shooting up from the ground sharp and clean like a periscope. The future was a separateness, it had a different consistency. At a certain altitude he could see the lake and the circular city at the foot of the Jura, a mountain whose crest he was able to sweep over daily. On the other side of its circumference, the city's core thickened with skyscrapers, then leveled, dissipating horizontally to scattered houses. He thought of the city he had lived in, of the cities he had imagined or heard of; how each of those cities had had its own personality, a personality he had forced himself to know; but now they were all basically the same, and only the personality of people seemed to him mutable and significant. He kept the plane on an ascent of only a few degrees, flying at the minimum of wing resistance, with next to no flutter. Perhaps living in such a neutral, ill-defined city, because the city is international, makes people more involved. Fifteen minutes into his flight he looks down at the airfield and the hangar. Incredible, that soon he will return, he and his plane, to that half barrel that seems so little from above. He looks at the runway, at the figure leaving the runway and walking toward the main building, its head turned up. On the instrument panel, the gas gauge is only half empty, so he thinks, "Why not take another short spin?"

4

Brahe went to the young woman at the rental office and told her what happened. She pursed her lips and said, "That's hard for us to believe."

Besides the office there was only a small bar in the hall, and the bartender could hardly have been among the persons making that judgment. Brahe asked, "Us?" She shrugged, then returned the passbook to him, without any charge for flight time.

Outside there was a whirring, a low hum; Brahe ran out onto the glass-enclosed terrace just in time to see the Zlin approach the runway. As it descended, its nose appeared to be looking for the best spot on the ground. It was landing like a sharpshooter.

In the split second that the Zlin touched down, regaining complete control of itself, Brahe saw the pilot's profile against the light: the man was in the back seat, perhaps to have a better center of gravity, and the canopy was half-open. He landed quickly and taxied to the end of the runway.

In front of the hangar Brahe regarded the man still seated in the Zlin, with the engine turned off: white hair, a wide face, a plaid flannel shirt opened at the collar. He thumbed the instruments, turning off switches, then released the seatbelt, slid out onto the wing, picked up his jacket from the front seat, and dropped to the ground.

"You must be crazy," said Brahe, taking one step forward. He said this slowly, like a statement of fact.

Epstein looked at the young man, observed a tall, wide bone structure. He said, "Excuse me?"

"Only a madman would pass so low over the field."

"So it was you." Epstein smiled. "I didn't think you

5

would wait for me." He went to the tail of the plane, and with his arms straight and hands together he lifted and tilted it into a balanced position. He started to push.

"If there had been any air traffic controllers," Brahe said, his hands in his pockets as the man pushed, "they would have taken away your license."

Epstein put the tail wheel back on the ground, catching his breath. "Yes, those people are strict."

"Besides," Brahe said when the pushing resumed, "I might have crashed."

Epstein turned his eyes on the young man. "You don't look the type." He craned his neck to see if the wings were clearing the hangar doors. "In any event," he said with a smile, "if you're trying to punish me by not helping me bring the plane inside, I must tell you that a Zlin is extremely light." In the hangar, he turned the plane by holding onto the fuselage to swing the nose forward, tail end toward the wall, and positioned it between the others.

The Zlin disappeared under the tarpaulin; Epstein let the cloth fall over the tail and wings. Brahe asked, "Why a Zlin?"

Epstein gestured at the outline wrapped in white nylon: "You don't like them?"

"I mean, why an aerobatic plane?"

"Of course I don't do aerobatics. But the controls are very responsive, and it climbs quickly." He turned away one more time, to make sure that everything was in order. "I've had it several years."

Now they are face to face, unable to avoid each other's eyes. Brahe's eyes are dark, his brows circumflexes. Epstein, his jacket in his folded arms, moves sideways, begins to walk in front of the row of planes, passes the new Pipers, Cessnas, the SIAI Marchettis, and stops by an old streamlined violet and beige twin engine with high wings and the engines hanging underneath. "Have you seen this?"

"The Dornier?" Brahe approached the plane.

Epstein nodded. "It makes a strange noise when it runs, like crackling paper."

"That's the Lycomings," said Brahe, pointing to the engines. "Their cylinders are parallel; that's why they don't roar like radial engines."

Epstein turned to look at the young man but said nothing. He continued walking.

Gray light filtered through the long half-vaulted window, illuminating the fuselages. The planes had been arranged by the mechanic according to the frequency of use. The farther one went from the two huge sliding doors, the older the models became. Enclosed, removed from their function, they made an eerie impression. "Like furniture," Epstein said. "In the States once, I visited a friend at McDonnell Douglas. There was a newly completed DC8, an enormous plane in an enormous hangar. A fuselage nested in scaffolding. The workmen were painting PAN AMERICAN with cutout letters and a spraygun. It was fast-drying paint. They removed the stencils from the fuselage and held them upright: the I in AMERICAN was so large, a workman could walk through it without stooping. As if it were a door. It was strange to see the plane at that level, from that point of view, in an enclosed place and so near."

They passed a De Havilland with its fixed undercarriage and its skis, slightly raised, next to the wheels. It was a single-engine plane, but bigger than the others, with a three-bladed propeller and several little windows in the hull. "Did you ever land on ice?" asked Brahe.

"No," said Epstein. "Did you?"

"You do it by using the flaps and the engine. Otherwise you'll never come to a stop," Brahe said, making a long gesture with his arm.

"That makes sense. And you've done it?"

"No," said the young man, smiling for the first time. They walked together, though not in any particular direction, passing from plane to plane the way one changes subjects in a conversation. And you couldn't really say that they were walking together, not yet anyway, but each followed or anticipated the other, and their words converged or diverged as did their movements in space. "Airplanes," said Epstein, "are perfection personified, but a little forbidding, like animals. A plane is nothing like a bird. It has a long nose, and haunches in the rear, like a dog or cat." Brahe nodded, looking at a sea-blue Grumman Hellcat, at the small red plates on the rim of the wing they had used to close off the machine-gun vents.

Epstein ambled easily, surveying the planes as though he knew each one personally. "The curious thing is that the basic principles are the same for all of them, often down to the dimensions and proportions, yet every plane has its own characteristics, its own defects, even its own voice. The last De Havilland has the same slightly smooth heaviness as the first, even though over the years the designers, technicians, and perhaps even the manufacturers have changed. You want to try them all, these planes, and when you're inside one that you're unaccustomed to, the smallest differences are momentarily baffling: the foot rests lower on the pedal, the stick is stiffer in your hand, the ceiling of the cockpit is higher. The eye cannot find the altimeter at first, it searches for it. It sees the instrument then, instead of automatically registering numbers and arrows. And the hands and feet feel the physical reality of the controls, the material of which the controls are made, controls that normally operate without our awareness of them. The plane banks, but with less use of the rudder; or perhaps you have to gun the engine more; and every movement in space outside no longer quite corresponds to what you do inside. The experience is not as natural, as immediate, and for the first time it comes home to you that you're really flying."

Brahe put a finger to his eyebrow, smiled, and looked at Epstein. "Yes. That's how it is. And then you quickly become accustomed to the differences." Increasing his pace, he came to a hulk covered with rough brown canvas. He said, "This is perhaps the most beautiful of all." He lifted the canvas, and dappled colors of sand and green appeared: a camouflage that, breaking the contour of the wings, imparted a sinuousness to the fundamental geometries. The canvas, half off, now fell completely, and the tear-shaped top of a Spitfire Supermarine appeared, its rear-view mirror mounted on the outside, at the edge, to enable the pilot to see behind the tail. It had a low arrowlike fuselage with blunt-curved wings and a white-and-blue belly to make it invisible from the ground, and there were side doors for unloading.

"It belongs to the mechanic," said Brahe. "He bought it at an auction. He wants to recondition it, I think."

"If he can find the parts," said Epstein. He walked along it slowly. "It's the most streamlined, cleanest thing they were able to build around a pilot at that time. It traveled more than five hundred kilometers an hour and with only one engine."

"A Rolls-Royce," said Brahe.

"What do you mean, a Rolls-Royce? The Spitfire had a Bristol."

"I don't think so. The Bristols were rotary engines, they could be overtaken by Halifaxes, by Lancasters, the big bombers."

Epstein laid his jacket on the wing, took his glasses from his shirt pocket and put them on, and near the engine stood on tiptoe. Head over the propeller, he looked inside for the serial number. Then slowly fell back onto his heels. He removed his glasses and said smiling, without looking at Brahe, "The only Spitfire in history with a Rolls engine." There were footsteps. Brahe and Epstein turned. Brahe quickly pulled the canvas over the Spitfire.

A thin young woman approached. Her slacks were wide at the hip and narrow at the ankles. She was looking among the planes, then saw the two men. In a voice too loud for the distance between them she said, "Have you seen the mechanic?"

Epstein and Brahe walked toward her, entering the square of light at the hangar's doorway. Brahe said, "He went into town, but he should be back by noon."

"I'm here," said the young woman.

Brahe looked at her the way a young man looks at a young woman, and said, "Hello."

She smiled, tilting her head: "I mean it's my turn. I'm supposed to take the Cessna up and I don't know if it's ready." She pointed to the plane that Brahe had been in a short time before.

They all went out to the plane, Epstein a little removed from the other two. "I think there's something wrong with its undercarriage," Brahe said. He moved his eyes from the craft to Epstein, not pointedly, but only out of curiosity. Epstein had predicted this look a second before he turned to face Brahe; he had a faint, impassive smile. The girl murmured as she consulted her watch.

Brahe explained that he had made a hard landing, but didn't give the reason. "The landing gear might be damaged." The young woman listened with her hands at her waist, glancing at Epstein every now and then.

Epstein thought about how each of their positions—the distances between them, and between them and the plane, which each of them again contemplated—instantaneously suggested ideas, perspectives, and awarenesses of self and of the other, all of which took place privately, beneath phrases like "Let's hope he gets here soon" or "There may be nothing wrong with the gear, but why take chances?" This perception, he thought, like a scaffold held a person upright, and if it ceased, the person would crumble, like one who is decapitated while walking and whose body continues to take a step or two before falling. He smiled and said, "I think it's all right." They left the young woman stroking the propeller.

They proceeded to the main building, passed a fuel pump housed in a round shelter, and followed a row of short lime trees along the fence, walking in silence, each in his own way struck by the quality of the light and the air. Brahe said, "Perhaps you still owe me an explanation."

After a long pause, as if giving the question serious thought, Epstein said calmly but decidedly, "No, I don't believe so."

At the gate they saw the mechanic's pickup truck. Slowing down, the mechanic looked at Brahe, and then, bending even lower over the steering wheel, took a long look at Epstein, then again at Brahe, as if to say, "Now what?" Brahe would have waved, but thought the gesture might annoy Epstein.

Epstein put on his jacket, adjusted it, lowered the thick wool collar, ran a hand over his straight white hair. He touched Brahe on the shoulder and said, "I'll buy you a juice."

The bar in the main room was already filled with people sitting in lounge chairs in front of the windowed terrace, talking animatedly. Above the long mirror at the counter, a clock without numerals showed a quarter after nine. "Is it late for you?" asked Epstein. The young man shook his head, catching the reflection of his shaking head in the mirror.

This airport no longer has scheduled flights. Its furnishings are old but well-preserved, and on one wall there is a planisphere divided vertically by sky-blue metal lines indicating time zones. "See," said Epstein, pointing at the panel with his glass: "Time zones like that are useless. The partitioning should be not by hours but by actions. For example, from Tokyo to Buenos Aires all those who at this moment are drinking raspberry juice or rubbing their chins, or looking at a clock and thinking that somewhere else it's a different hour, should be linked. More lines would be needed, intersecting from all directions, according to the specific action. That way, no one would have to wonder who is doing, just then, the exact same thing that he is doing. Which can be, sometimes, an overwhelming desire, like a lust for conspiracy."

Brahe pressed a finger to his eyebrow, thinking how such an idea could best be realized. "You would have to create a set of all actions, and choose subsets on the basis of simultaneity and similarity."

"Actions of joy," Epstein reflected, "even if mild, but of joy." And he looked at a framed poster of a tri-engine Swissair in flight above a man riding a camel in the desert.

Out of one of the former offices of the airline company the young woman from the rental office appeared; she went to the bar where Brahe and Epstein were drinking. Epstein turned and smiled. "Oh, so you've met!" she said, looking at Brahe with interest, but gravitating more toward Epstein, almost as if assuming his point of view. "This young man wanted very much to talk to you." "Yes," said Brahe, finishing his drink. The woman held a pastel-blue flight manual with a worn binding; she handed it to Epstein, who quickly pocketed it. Taking a more balanced position between the two, as if reappraising them, she said, "All right, I'm leaving." When she left, Epstein finished his drink and said, "Ira Epstein," with a slight ironic bow.

"Pietro Brahe," Brahe said.

"You're Italian."

"Italian."

"An Italian with a car?" asked Epstein, squinting.

"Depends how far," Brahe said, realizing the question was about distances.

"Bellerive, on the right side of the lake."

They entered the city from the west, taking a main road that cut across wide avenues where gleaming banks and jewelry shops reflected the blue above, as well as the long shape of their car as it stopped at lights or moved in the fluid, orderly traffic. Cars turned corners slowly, or else filed by as straight as if they were on rails, the drivers so calm and safe that the diagonal straps of their seatbelts seemed like military sashes. They crossed the big bridge, from where one could see everything, the city, the shore, Mont Blanc. Viewed from above, the bridge was a final thread that sewed together the two shores of the Rhone before the river flowed into the lake.

Opposite the English Garden, just past the bridge, Epstein said, "Turn here, then go straight."

When he had climbed into the large blue station wagon, he noticed that inside there was not a scrap of paper on the floor or a newspaper on the seat, or any personal belongings. He read the notice on the dashboard that informed drivers as to proper tire pressure and the mileage recommended between oil changes. He asked, "You're not working today?"

"What makes you think I work?" said Brahe, smiling.

"Italian in Geneva, with company car. You work at the merry-go-round?"

14

Looking from the rear-view to the side-view mirror, Brahe accelerated to pass. "Yes, I work at the merry-go-round."

"And what exactly do you do there?"

"I keep an eye out for the children. When they visit, I take photographs to prove that they have indeed visited." Brahe moved back into his lane.

Cruising along the left shore, they passed the quays and the vertical jet of water which wavered in the wind as it fell endlessly. "As long as I've been here," said Epstein, regarding the geyser behind Brahe's profile, "I've grown used to everything except that fountain. It's like the totem of a primitive civilization that discovered a thermal spring. The idea of a liquid monument isn't bad, raised in the morning and lowered at night; but how can one take seriously a thing that all over the world is hello in tugboat language?"

"A monument to water," Brahe said, scanning the huge white mountain on the horizon, "is appropriately made of water."

"Yes, water is vital. Sleep, too. Fundamental." But he spoke as though thinking about something else, so his use of "fundamental" was unclear. They turned up a small drive bathed in warm light, which led to the lake, between houses surrounded by low walls topped with planters full of zinnias, asclepiases, and snapdragons. At the last gate, its grille in rhombuses, Epstein said, "Here."

For a silent moment they observed the edifices of peace and collectivism on the opposite shore of the lake, the large white marble palace in the limpid April morning.

"You go flying on Thursdays?" Epstein asked.

"It varies. It's not up to me," replied Brahe.

There was a metallic hum, and the gate lowered, disappeared into the ground. Epstein opened the car door but didn't get out. Brahe saw long glass doors leading to a garden, a scene reminiscent of Japan.

Epstein tapped the dashboard. "I'm in the phonebook. But you, if someone wanted to talk airplanes with you?"

"Call the merry-go-round, ask for the French line."

Tall and calm, Brahe sped back along the lakeshore drive, crossed the city, ascended eastward. He took the underpass beneath the main runway of the city airport; above him a yellow-and-amaranth jumbo jet was landing with a roar. Then straight, a stretch of fields of rape and poppies; then, without stopping, a nod to the customs officer. His attention wandered, his thoughts were vague, with a sudden nostalgia sometimes felt not only for what has happened but also for what is yet to happen. Before he knew it, he was in Ferney-Voltaire. In the driveway that led to his house he shifted into first gear, then into neutral in the garage.

On the patio, Eileen, the English girl who built magnets, and Sarad, the Indian who worked on gravitational waves, looked at Brahe without leaving their deck chairs.

"We were out here all morning waiting for you to fly over," said Eileen, shading her face with her hand.

Brahe touched his eyebrow. "Sorry, but I didn't go up. I was taking off when a guy above me missed me by a hair and forced me down."

"You're not hurt?" she asked, scrutinizing him.

16

"No, nothing happened," Brahe said, smiling. "Then I talked with him a while. An interesting guy. Ira Epstein."

"Ira Epstein?" Eileen turned to Sarad, then looked at Brahe again. "How old is he?"

"I have no idea. He has white hair."

"It must be the writer." Eileen got up from her chair.

Brahe, silent, shrugged, but the Indian said, "Is Epstein still alive?" as he closed his book.

The pain returned at the same hour the following day. Many meters underground, while showing his colleagues the chart of a subatomic collision, Brahe felt a twinge of pain in the small of his back, but it quickly diffused into a general tingling, as if the body were celebrating a personal observance.

2

At dawn, the last image was no different from what Brahe had observed at the beginning of the night. On the dark monitor there appeared, first, a frame with the series number, code, and time of the experiment. Then, from left to right, rapid lines. Those that intersected at the center, where the impact was, generated other lines, continuous or dotted. Curves, parabolas, ellipses, tiny vortices that coiled around themselves. For a time they remained in place, frozen, poised, then it began again. Every ten seconds, the notes of the diapason descended and died, the numbers hit their limit, and the screen blew into blackness. Brahe knew the past and future of each line. The ideal would have been a new line, a line which, though probable, would be where no line had been before. The visualization as a whole suggested a metropolis at night seen from above, roads with red and white stripes, moving headlights, or an electronic control board, or colored gems on a jeweler's black velvet. The images did not represent the entire event, but only that part of it that would reveal the thing that was new. The totality of the event, of the night's millions of events, was stored in the memory.

Rüdiger, the German, wearing salmon-pink pants and a striped shirt, said from his table, "Nothing on the screen."

Brahe checked the communications monitor that hung from the ceiling and said, "Call the center. See if there's been an interruption."

Rüdiger, waiting to get through, hummed the descending notes they had listened to all night: "blin blin blin blun." Then, the message on the phone. Finally he hung up and said, "Complication. They start up again tomorrow at eleven."

"Then we're finished," sighed Brahe, and he imagined the few people in the other rooms along thirty kilometers of halls, all underground, in a ring that linked their gestures and intentions. Probably now, too, the others were leaning back in their chairs, stretching their arms, rubbing their eyes.

At his desk Brahe jotted in his log the night's results: nothing new. Rüdiger placed a hand on Brahe's shoulder; he waited for him to sign his name and then with a smile whispered, "Nothing new? With all we saw last night?"

"But let's not tell them yet," said Brahe with the same smile. "We'll keep it to ourselves, then make a sensational announcement."

"Ah, the fiendish Doctor Brahe!" said Rüdiger, going over to the console.

Brahe closed the log, leaving the pen in the seam, and clasped his hands behind his neck. The blond German was removing index cards from the cabinet, checking both sides and refiling them. He sighed, then slumped to show fatigue. For Brahe's amusement. Brahe remembered the first time he met Rüdiger. At the North Pole. In two separate Plexiglas observation domes about ten feet apart, they could communicate only by phone, but Rüdiger, from his bubble, began to speak to him in sign language, touching ears and eyes, forming letters with his fingers, inside the bubble, the blue sky in the background.

"You should take one of these," Rüdiger said, offering the multiple male plug he had just detached from the cable. "And the female, too."

Brahe gave a little nod. He thinks of their friendship, of that strange intimacy that comes from working together in isolation like this, through nights like this, in vast silent rooms like this, among huge machines, and insulated from the radiation by thick concrete blocks. They do not talk about their work except when absolutely necessary. Everything they say is understood as between gentlemen, with allusions, gestures, a conceptual shorthand that little by little reduces the greatest complexity to a single word.

In the tunnel that crossed the ring there were zones more roughhewn and zones where the floor and wall panels made interiors of blue-white light, with the background noise of the air conditioning, the coolers for the magnets, the fans. In the tunnel, the air was not air, and thoughts like "two in the morning" or "four in the afternoon" were totally irrelevant, time being represented only by sequences of numbers, numbers no different from those that indicated, on the screen, the birth and death of the lines.

"Coming?" Brahe asked, slipping on his jacket.

"No, I'll be a while longer," Rüdiger answered. "I want to go over what happened tonight."

"We saw what there was to see," Brahe said slowly. "There was nothing."

The German shrugged, fingering the plug.

Brahe felt they had reached the point where fatigue becomes so subtle and fluid, that to continue seems less tiring, less difficult than to leave. "Careful," he said with a smile to lighten the atmosphere.

At the end of the room he stopped at the foot of the detector, a tall and massive structure beneath the concrete vault, with its castle of bridges and catwalks on different levels. Brahe thought of the ring that passed through the heart of this machine, of the flow within the ring, but now the flow had stopped, and what was hidden in the flow. He gave one last look and turned, nodding to Rüdiger, who was at the computer retrieving the data from the memory.

Then Brahe was going up in the elevator, staring at walls of metal and then walls of concrete, and then a sparkling surface of quartz and feldspar, which contained fossils, perhaps of the small *Lycoteras loricatum,* or some other radiolarian or echinoderm of the Jurassic, the period that took its name from these Jura mountains, in whose bowels he was at that moment. Then he was ascending through the stratum of moraine, limestone and rocks deposited by glaciation, and then he was up in the stratum of the roots of broadleafs and conifers that rose from the forest floor to the first light of dawn.

His car was cold. He ran the engine. Then he sped

through the growing brightness. The headlights met fog first thick then patchy. After a few miles he stopped in Echenevex at a corner café. Getting out, he noticed that his radiation film-badge was still clipped to his collar. He removed it, put it in his pocket.

Eating a croissant and drinking a cup of coffee, he said something to the manager, whom he knew. The manager said, "Too true. We're the changing of the guard on the border of sleep." Brahe went to the window with his cup and croissant; on the opposite sidewalk were several people waiting for the first bus, looking as if they just got out of bed.

Quickly he passed through Chevry, Vaux, Bretigny, and Previssin, where the scattered houses of the French countryside were clumped along the filaments of roads and the nodes of towns. He arrived in Ferney-Voltaire at that false hour when it is light though the sun has not yet risen. The silence in his house was the active silence of sleepers. He went to the top floor and found on the desk of his studio a note from Eileen: "Cesare and Palmiro arriving from Italy with the mozzarella. Coming for brunch. Do you want to be awakened?" He looked at Eileen's upward and rightward handwriting, then went down to the kitchen and scrawled on the small black-board: "Wake me up!"

Lying on the couch, he tried to find a reason, or an image, to prompt sleep, but as soon as he closed his eyes, the computer dots appeared, almost like phosphenes. He considered the objects around him, and came to the ceiling fan, whose blades he imagined in a vertical position. If he held the propeller motionless with his hands, the fuselage would start to rotate in the opposite direction, and from there he arrived at Epstein. He was interested, and sleep retreated, but then a message flashed, at first meaningless. It was repeated: "Saturday at two o'clock." Again he saw his blood circulating, and the message reappeared as "Saturday at two o'clock, Mr. Wang," and then reappeared for the last time, concluding with, "Today is Saturday," and Brahe woke completely and exclaimed, "God."

At his desk under the half-moon window, he removed the file folder with the label DEUS, unfastened the clip, and took out the blueprint of a machine to be built in a few years. Faint, broken lines indicated the connections between the different parts built by the different groups in the different countries. Brahe's part was next to Wang's. The problem was that Wang wanted twenty more centimeters, as he had telexed. The young man had searched and rearranged but came to the conclusion that that was impossible. The only solution was to falsify the blueprint. Take twenty centimeters out of Wang's sector, then "give" them back. He looked closer at the blueprint: there would be no trouble erasing lines, but whiting them out would also white out the fine blue dust of the background. He contemplated some involved photocopying; he rested his cheek on the sheet of paper, checking its porosity and the detail of the background. Up close, the lines of the detector appeared thick, though only the ones farthest away were in focus. A thick orange line rose from the edge of the table toward the window and the roofs, not distant, of Castle Voltaire. With his cheek on the blueprint, Brahe saw the sun rise, then saw nothing more.

3

Mail delivery can be thought of as warfare, an invasion. Advertising fliers, circulars land on a beachhead, foot soldiers with no time to test themselves or their equipment. Fliers written indifferently and sent to indifferent readers. Fliers saying only that they have arrived. They are silent, often even stampless, a postal illusion based on the naked fact of their delivery. A crime, to send them that way. Bills and financial reports, though of the same category, are put in better cells because of their greater importance. Envelopes from the draft board, still higher in the pecking order, require kid gloves. But the true heroes of this paper army are the personal envelopes, the real letters—to be read immediately, the first time with the heart or in homage to their calligraphy; a second time, slowly, taking in the parenthetical phrases. Some remain unopened for days or longer, until the uneasy feeling of not having opened them passes. In the end they remain like parachutists dropped outside the battle zone, with no enemy to fight.

Ira Epstein would answer his letters at once, then walk or drive to mail them from the post office. All his life, no matter in what city he lived, he did not trust mailboxes. Colorless, solitary, often off in some dead corner, a mailbox did not convey a sense of communication. And neither he nor anyone he knew had ever actually seen one being emptied by a mailman.

Epstein opens the envelope and immediately notices something wrong. The type, the margins are too neat. He turns quickly to the signature on the second page and discovers an infiltrator.

He reads the letter standing at the window, his glasses crooked on his face, as though he were unaccustomed to them. A slight smile breaks on his lips. He rereads, slowly now, without the glasses, then goes outside with the letter folded in his back pocket.

Following the cement tiles, which are arranged to create a winding path among swollen clumps of calycanthus and magnolia, he walks with folded arms, back straight, as though on an increasingly intricate conveyor belt. Finally, crossing gravel and ground subtly raked, he reaches the far end of the villa, where he sits on a bamboo deck chair by a small white table. He looks at the United Nations Building beyond the road, then in a writing pad writes:

My Dear Ed:
You're amazing. In civilian clothes your letter passed the front lines and reached its target. But it changes nothing. You will have no new book "for the American market," you will

have no new book at all. If the big prize comes, it will be for what I have done up to now. Otherwise, forget it. I'm sure you understood that perfectly when we talked last fall. You're the scrupulous type who carries out his obligations to the end. And so am I. But I have fulfilled my obligations, at least those that involve you. (Which does not mean that you are "only my publisher.") But I have a different obligation now to carry out, and this will separate us for the first time. Since you officially ask about this, I will give you an official reply, in order to talk to you unofficially afterward.

For me there has been no transition period, no second thoughts. Nothing to mull over in the sense you mean. I worked for thirty years with a passion, wrote every day, drank large quantities of water and passed large quantities of water, assuring me excellent kidney function. I was happy, really happy, even in the worst moments, when a writer feels that a book is abandoning him, evading him, and he becomes so depressed that everything seems the same and even a paragraph is beyond him. Then, the next morning, the book rejoins him, and it is as if nothing happened. I believe I can say that I have experienced writing in all its forms, in all its possibilities. Today, I am free of it, with joy. I always wished, all my life, that writing and storytelling could be transparent for me, too. Now that the moment has arrived, I don't intend to ruin it. In short, I have reached the side opposite to the side I entered many years ago, when I brought you my first manuscript.

Consider one who digs a hole in Alaska, and keeps digging. Does he emerge in Antarctica feetfirst? But if the bottom remains the bottom and the top the top, what of the law of gravity? Or does the digger turn upside down at the center of the earth, where the temperature is most like hell? But what space would there be for him to turn upside down, if the tunnel is the same diameter as he? And, assuming he turns, is he aware of it? What does he feel? I really don't know yet how I emerged, headfirst or feetfirst. But I emerged. I am on the other side. And here there is everything to see, and I am just beginning.

You once said I was an extraordinary self-manager "in such an instinctive, animal way that everything can be forgiven you." Well, I will not manage my old age by rearranging or recycling what I've already done. For the same reason, I've decided against making the tour again of our foreign cultural centers, academies, foundations. Certainly I owe you that, but I've done it for years with commitment and responsibility, accompanying my books like a salesman, though a salesman of what product I know not. What I've written does not belong to me, and I'm only the first of my readers: this was what I tried to explain in my lectures. But if I drank with my left hand, someone at the table would say, "With the left! Like Caleb!"—referring to that asymmetrical character in my book. People would look at my hands, my watch, my eyebrows, the way I walked. I was compared to all sorts of literary things. It is strange when distinctions are no longer made between books and people. But I carried on.

Last year, I was introduced with that same old nickname: "Little Eagle." Ed! I'm over sixty. I laughed and clapped like a monkey. But I'm tired of TV interviewers (especially intelligent ones like Herbert Wheeler) who suddenly turn pale and purse their lips. Thinking he was unwell, I took his hand in mine. But he raised his head and said, syllable by syllable, "What is the universe according to Epstein?" There was a time, I would have changed the subject, looked for a ploy, something to minimize that question, that situation, the universe, and myself. Today, I don't want to bother.

It may be interesting how my relationship with ethics and esthetics has changed from book to book (though you have always spoken of my "cynical candor"). But I have no time to rethink and reunderstand my past. I'm too busy with my present. (Which is not "life," I've lived enough.) My present is a note on a scale, a long, clear note in harmony with all the others, and with my new ambition, my fantasy, to see beyond form. . . . And on this cryptic note I send you my salutations and farewell, dear friend.

Yours, Ira.

Epstein pauses, turns the pages of his writing pad with his thumb, assessing the length of the letter. Too long? But where to cut it? Reading it again, he remembers this is Saturday. If he cuts the letter, he'll have to copy it over. Let it be. He folds the sheets in three for the envelope.

With an arm stretched above his head, he now looks at the yard that extends down to the fence, to the lake: trees with twigs and branches, beds of flowers arranged symmetrically and in progressions of color, to relax the senses. And in fact he feels relaxed. Yet he reflects that there are rules for pruning, watering, and trimming, rules of perspective, of light and shadow, and horticultural techniques, the proportions of compost and peat, that only his gardener knows. Mortifying, to benefit from a thing, even when the benefit is simply relaxation, without perceiving the ideas behind it. Selecting flowers for his novels, he always paid attention to their phonetics. Mahonia, for instance, might fit in a sentence better than violet, convolvulus better than honeysuckle, verbena better than tulips. But then, having finished the book, and as he was revising it, he would learn that mahonia was highly resistant to cold, but what was the point of such resistance if the plant was stuck in a story set in the tropics? Epstein built gardens in his books by matching flowers' names and colors, then later checked their plausibility. That was one of the ways he learned. But he could not apply this system to machines or animals. A character with such-and-such a temperament had to drive such-and-such a car. On a particular horizon there had to be a particular animal. Once an editor complained, "Look, in Seattle there are no bullet thistles." Epstein said, "Well, put in any plant you like. Whatever they have in Seattle."

He concentrates again on the chromatics in his garden. Just as the quaver is an undulation of sound, so colors, from violet to red, have their frequencies and wavelengths. Correspondences of this kind have been a part of his work. But now they offer themselves differently, more intimate and shaded, less purposeful.

Finally he goes to his car in the garage, backs out of the villa, and steers onto Quai Gustave Ador, along the shore and the boats. He passes cars, crossing the double yellow line, to reach the post office before it closes.

4

Before Brahe could turn his head or close his mouth, Eileen was at his side, waking him. He opened his eyes. The window was divided into two colors at the horizon: the yellow green of the fields, the gray-white blue of the sky. He saw the girl, glanced at his watch, and jumped up from the chair, so suddenly that someone inside him, in compensation, slowly closed his eyes again. Eileen turned away for a moment to give him time to collect himself. She said, half-scolding, half-casually, "It's better to sleep at night."

Brahe smiled and took a deep breath. "Are Cesare and Palmiro here yet?"

"No, but Sarad has prepared everything in the yard."

Brahe nodded, back at his table. In his sleep he'd creased a paper. He smoothed it with his finger and said, "I don't believe I can stay for breakfast."

In an interested-uninterested way Eileen came over and looked at the blueprint. Brahe told her about it and his appointment with Mr. Wang. "A shark," she said.

"For his twenty centimeters more he's coming specially from Berlin." Brahe showed her the junction between the two parts of the detector.

She bent over the blueprint, tall and broad-shouldered in her baggy sweater. "Can we give them to him?"

Brahe shook his head, hands in his pockets. "I checked everything last night. There's not enough space. I'll have to give them to him without giving them to him."

"Not correct procedure," Eileen said, an eyebrow arched over a pale eye. "And not too easy, knowing Wang."

"I'll move my part twenty centimeters over," Brahe said, hands parallel, as though marking a threshold, "and then pretend to give that to him when we discuss the problem." In a lower voice, he added, "It's not my fault the profession is getting like that."

"Doesn't Wang have a copy?"

"This is the only blueprint. He has the general measurements of the machine and the detail of his own part. I can move lines, but the problem is the dust, the background."

"You mean the noise?" she asked, using the language of physics.

"Yes, the noise."

Eileen took the drawing from the table, examined it closely, then turned it over and held it up to the light. "What we need is ink, fountain-pen ink." Brahe opened a drawer and pulled out a small box. She removed the cap from the bottle inside and put a drop on her finger, checking the opacity. "How much time do we have?"

"An hour, at most. Then I have to leave," Brahe said, looking at his watch.

Eileen's expression was attentive, with a hint of irony. She wiped her finger on the box, considered Brahe, then the blueprint, then Brahe again, with his tousled hair and puffy eyes. She said, "We definitely need coffee. I'll bring some up. In the meantime, you mark the area with a pencil."

Brahe sat again at the table when Eileen left the room. He drew in lines, whited out others. Although he used the liquid sparingly and the brush was very thin, on the blueprint three white frames now broke the dustlike surface of the background, as if the new elements in pencil hung suspended, apart from the rest. Brahe wondered if the drawing could be saved.

He washed up, changed his clothes. In the bathroom he thought about the importance of water: Epstein had talked about that. Then, he became aware that his thoughts went on like open curves in space, never coming to an end. He breathed in strange slow motion, as though still asleep, and his movements were only the background to his thoughts. He recovered with an inner click, accelerated, and focused on the toothbrush, the shaver, the sponge.

When he returned to his study, Eileen was already seated at the table. He stopped at the door, watched for a second. The curve of her back, her shoulders silhouetted against the moon-shaped window. Then he, too, sat at the table, but sideways, not to distract her.

Eileen had diluted the ink, making several tests to obtain the right color; then she had retraced the lines of the pencil. With a needle dipped into the blue ink she now put dots, extremely tiny and seemingly at random, all over the white frames and around the new lines of the blueprint. Little by little the dots became not dots but merged into the embroidery of noise, the fabric that Eileen was repairing, making seamless.

"You're very clever." Brahe smiled, admiring her: she, absorbed in the drawing, lips pursed, a wisp of hair almost touching the sheet, and eyes extraordinarily green.

She replied in Italian, without looking up. "A theoretician like you should expect manual finesse from one who builds magnets." Her consonants were liquid, but anything would have been liquid on her tongue.

"I was sure of it. Otherwise I wouldn't have asked you." But Brahe thought, instead, of the mystery of freehand drawing; that, unpredictable and rule-eluding, like sewing, it belonged to the domain of women.

Sometimes Eileen touched the sheet with the needle hardly wetted, other times she took a bigger drop, using less color. After applying it, she pulled the paper's edges until the surface absorbed the drop in a misty blue. Now and then she leaned back to see the whole effect.

Brahe poured coffee into her cup. He drank, standing at the window. The tiny blue dots, the young woman with her fine dark hair, the light, the situation, and he drinking coffee seem, though perceived in this instant, to come from his future or perhaps that he is in that future remembering them.

She regarded him for a moment, the needle in her hand. "Pietro Brahe, you're one of those who are moved only by their work." She said it slowly.

"Not really," he smiled, tense. "It's more than that."

Eileen gave the blueprint a last look: the background was again whole, and the newness of the detector's lines undetectable. "This is a great forgery at Wang's expense."

Brahe bent over the paper: "Remarkable."

"It would be better if you made a Xerox," she said, standing up. "That way, absolutely nothing will show."

The noise of tires on gravel, slamming doors, and greetings could be heard. "They've arrived. I'll go down," she said.

At his door he stopped her, lightly touched her arm. "I don't know how to thank you," he said. She smiled at him and left.

Brahe looked at his watch, and realized that he was late. He ran into the bedroom, took a jacket from his closet, but it didn't go with his trousers, then another, but that clashed with his shirt. One light jacket did match, but it was uncomfortable, too stiff. Finally he took a leather jacket, a little too tight, and a briefcase he never used before. He looked at the blueprint one last time, then folded it. The detector, when its calorimeters and scintillometers were encased in plastic and the cables were covered up, would assume the shape of a shoe-polishing machine: the motor at the center and a circular brush on either side, one to apply the polish and the other for buffing. It would be as high as the three-story house with stairs that Brahe was now descending.

On the patio he welcomed Cesare and Palmiro, logicians who always worked as a team. They said, "Pietro, you absolutely have to stay—this time it's terrific!"

"What's terrific?"

"The mozzarella," Sarad answered for all present, as if Indians, too, were connoisseurs of cheese.

Eileen was cutting thin slices of prosciutto and salami, arranging them on trays with little open sandwiches of pâté

34

and lettuce leaves. The rounds of mozzarella, traditionally brought by anyone returning from Italy, would be cut up in chunks. Brahe would have liked to stay, since he was hungry and occasions like this constituted, for him, "normalcy," being a desirable "waste of time." At first he had had to discipline himself to appreciate such situations. In the process he discovered that it was possible to converse without the need to convince or dominate, that companionship did not always have to be determined by work, and this, as he told Rüdiger once, made people "more rounded, larger."

But he had to leave, he said. He had an appointment with Mr. Wang.

Cesare and Palmiro: "The shark!"

Brahe nodded, smiling, cut the little ball at the top of the mozzarella and popped it into his mouth. As everyone yelled, "Come on, stay!" he left the patio, almost running, and called to Palmiro in Italian, "Move your car, I really have to go."

Like everyone else, Brahe had a double image of the land he now traversed. The giant underground ring extended to the Jura mountains, where the slope was a few degrees; it passed beneath ten small towns with church steeples and monuments, and the towns gave their names to the tunnel-halls below them. Brahe's conceptual topography was therefore circular, though roads connected all ten towns, as anywhere else, with straight diagonals deflected only by expropriated land, farms, natural hills, and rustic fences protecting fields of sunflowers and rape. Since the underground circularity did not correspond to the

35

geometry of the surface, Brahe, in order to go where he wanted, had to switch his mind from one mode to another, had to change the orientation of his imagination, and do it quickly, especially now that he was late, not having the time even to make a Xerox. He took a narrow asphalt road, cutting corners and skidding to arrive in Brétigny on time, the center of the ring, where the hotel was, for visitors, people not employed in the experiments.

Brahe left his car in the underground lot.

On the bulletin board he found a message for him from Mr. Wang: "Please come over to the rotunda." The hotel is a fairly tall building—cement stripes and glass cubes—alone in the countryside, surrounded by green meadow, a green unlike the other greens in the area. The stairs spiral around a glass house, and Brahe, climbing, can see the familiar date palm, the small Japanese trees, the bubbletop room half-hidden in the foliage with a plaque commemorating many experiments. This greenhouse is a glass nucleus within the glass nucleus of the hotel, a compounding of transparencies. On each floor, people of various ages and styles of clothing turn the pages of magazines in the light of the inside and outside windows; they drink at their tables while taking notes, they whisper to one another, they lean back in their red leather chairs.

Mr. Wang stood up when Brahe entered. He smiled and and with a slight bow said, "Thank you for coming." And, taking his hand, added, "So here you are"—as if after the telex, the appointment, the message left in the lobby, the encounter was a surprise.

"So here you are. Kind of you to come," Wang said, resuming his seat on the sofa that curved along the large rotunda under the open sky. "Very kind." Hands in his lap, he cast a penetrating look at Brahe. He repeated, "So here you are."

"Well, yes," said Brahe, looking for a place to put his briefcase. He sat facing Wang, stared at him, especially at the man's eyes. The irises, the large whites, the eyelids half-lowered.

"How is it going in Echenevex? I'm sure you've already seen something," Wang said.

"We've seen nothing yet."

"Oh, I'm sure you have. You've seen something, but you won't tell me."

"No." Brahe smiled. "We've just started. I assure you we've seen nothing." Afternoon light streamed through the glass vault, clean sunlight. Moving cars were visible, noiseless. Houses scattered among fields. The mountain in the background.

"With the power you have in your ring," Wang said, describing a circle in the air, "and with a detector like yours in Echenevex, I can't believe you've seen nothing. At least a candidate. But you wouldn't tell me, of course, until you were sure, until you checked and rechecked everything. Yes?" He waited for an answer, in the silence of the rotunda with only the two of them there. Waiting, he adjusted his tie, making the two strips more even, despite a poor knot or poor positioning. As his fingers worked, he looked at Brahe with liquid, patient eyes.

"Really, no." Brahe insisted. "You in Hamburg, I bet, can see much more than we here."

"Oh no. In Hamburg we see nothing, next to nothing," Wang said, giving up on his tie. "Nothing that hasn't already been seen."

A brief silence. Wang's gaze was at once distant and extremely close to Brahe, almost touching him. After a moment, he continued, "To see, one needs the energy to produce what one wants to see. Don't you think?"

Brahe shrugged. "Of course."

"To see, one needs much will and much energy."

Brahe nodded again. He tried to recall how many years it had taken Wang to win the Nobel Prize for seeing what he had seen. Yet the man did not look old. With his smooth hair on his thin face, with his lean body in his blue suit and white shirt, and the clashing tie, he appeared ageless.

"To see," Wang went on, "one needs great will and energy not during, but before and after, because when one sees the event, one does not see it while it is happening. The result must be anticipated, first, and interpreted, later." He stared at Brahe intensely and said, "You and I see this way."

As if Wang were hammering in one piton at a time. Before climbing to the next support, he carefully tested, with his foot, the support he was about to leave. Was it strong enough?

"If, to see," Wang said finally, "one needs the energy to produce what one wants to see, and if this energy is lacking, then it is impossible to see what one would like to see. That is a logical conclusion."

"Certainly," said Brahe.

"And so," Wang smiled as if quickly pulling in the rope, "I am grateful to you for giving the twenty centimeters I needed." And from his jacket he took a small diagram of his part of the detector.

"Wait a minute," Brahe said, unfolding his arms and putting out his hands. "In the telex I said we could discuss it. I did not say that I had given you the twenty centimeters."

With enormous dignity, leaning back, Wang looked at Brahe. "Discuss? But we have just discussed. Perhaps I did not make myself clear. To see, one—"

"Yes, yes," Brahe interrupted with a smile. "The will I have. The energy, too, I think. What I don't have is twenty centimeters."

"Why?"

"I would have to give up a line of hadron calorimeters, and I can't do that."

"You are making me very unhappy, Mr. Brahe." Wang looked away, at the view beyond the glass wall. Two young men passed, talking to one another in muted tones; they waved at Wang, who responded with a world-weary smile.

The physicist said to Brahe, in a different voice, "You see, I have come from Berlin expressly because of you. With the accelerator in Hamburg, my university position in Berlin, and many other things, my time is limited. I am trying to speed things up. There is never enough time, in our line of work. One races always to be first. That's why I am here, from Berlin. I'm relying on you. Now tell me the truth: in a machine so large, in a large section like yours, you can't spare twenty centimeters?" A deep look. "The truth, now."

Brahe spread his arms. "I don't want you to waste your

time. I've checked and double-checked, and there are not twenty centimeters available. But we can check together." From his briefcase he drew out the blueprint, opened it, handed it to Wang.

Wang studied the drawing, then said in a low voice, "A very beautiful machine. Very competitive."

Leaning over, Brahe pointed out with a pencil the broken and the unbroken lines, the shaded and the unshaded areas, which eventually would be plates and housings and units in series, elements thick and thin, peripherals in circles and squares, a tremendous, dense mass of material for the purpose of recording infinitesimal points of transient energy. Each part of the blueprint on which Brahe put his pencil, looking at Wang, was sensitive to one specific intensity and not another, to one specific amplitude, one specific velocity, duration, orientation, emanation. And yet the things to be seen were constantly interchangeable, protean, erasing their own distinctions. Consubstantiality alternating with identity.

Each part of the machine, of which Brahe gave the measurements, corresponded to a part of the event in its intersectings, impacts, ricochets, transitions, and transformations. Invisible entities in flux, like ideas. Each part, also, was designed and built by a different country. Countries in collaboration, connected by the lines of the blueprint yet set apart by boundaries well-marked, such as the boundary on which Brahe now stopped his pencil and said, "So you can see, it is practically impossible for me to move our equipment to the right by twenty centimeters."

"Practically," Wang said, "thus not absolutely." And brought the blueprint close to his eyes.

Brahe withdrew to a chair, put his elbows on the chair's arms, rested his chin on his hands. He observed the plants on the terrace around the rotunda, the nuances of the colors outside, green cement, blue panes, and the two young men murmuring on his right, and a girl who had just sat down with a book, and a plane high in the sky, above the vault, above all of them.

"You give yourself many margins." Wang pointed at precise places on the blueprint. "I understand, you want to be sure. But if you reduced by five millimeters the thickness of every plate, that would be enough. You keep all your units, and we have the twenty centimeters we need."

"*You* need," Brahe said, smiling, and looked at Wang's finger still on the drawing. "But then I lose definition."

"I don't think so." Wang began to examine the blueprint more carefully. He folded it, to concentrate on only one part; he held it flat; moved it; looked at it against the light; passed his finger over the paper and looked at his finger, then at the paper again. Finally he turned to Brahe and said, "Curious, here, the background."

"What?" Brahe asked.

"The background," Wang said, getting closer again to the paper. "You see the dots, the little dots? Here, all around these lines."

"Little dots?"

"Yes, these. In certain places they are denser, more packed. Some are even bigger."

Brahe smiled. "Really? To tell the truth, I never pay much attention to the background of a blueprint."

Wang pored over the drawing.

41

Brahe touched his eyebrow, following contiguous but different thoughts. He was an outside observer of the situation, not a part of it. He did not worry that it might affect his work adversely. He was simply curious.

"Incredible!" said Wang. He looked up at Brahe with a look that was naked, intense. Eyelids now fully open, the white around the irises striking.

Brahe felt he was completely transparent. "Forget the background," he said, "let's see what can be done." And with a smile, bending over, pencil point on the blueprint, he found the boundary line, drew two points to the right, one up, one down, then connected them with a line parallel to the line in the blueprint but about twenty centimeters from it, which virtually retraced the line that had been there before the revision and Eileen's forging of the background. Then, to Wang, "How's that?"

Wang blinked at the new line. "Yes, I think so," he said slowly. "I'll have to redo the calculations, but yes, I think that should be fine." He nodded. "Yes. Let me thank you. That's fine." He unfolded the blueprint, gave it one last look, then refolded it along the original creases and handed it back to Brahe. "We can make a Xerox of it before you leave?"

Hands back in his lap, eyes again half-lidded, Wang said, "You and I could do good work together. In a few years, when I come back with my German team and we start to build, you and I could do good work together. You won't regret the twenty centimeters you gave me."

Brahe nodded in agreement.

"And I will wait to hear from you," Wang went on, "as

soon as you finish the project in Echenevex. You will see something soon, assuming you haven't already seen something but don't want to tell me. You'll have news for me soon. You're young, you're smart, Signor Pietro Brahe. Very young, with many r's in your name."

"Thank you." The secret of the Chinese, Brahe thought, was repetition.

When they got up and collected their things, the two young men on their right acknowledged Wang with a slight bow, and the girl lifted her eyes from the book she was reading and looked at Brahe. Through the transparent vault, the sun was now less bright and more defined, lower among the intersecting struts that held the panes.

They went down a flight of stairs. In the lobby, at the base of the greenhouse, Wang looked back at the bubbletop half-hidden in the palms. He said, "Everything goes fast, everything moves so fast," perhaps thinking of his own name included on the brass plaque, with the date of the experiment.

Brahe drove quickly across the plain, entered the installation area, which was a circle on the south of the ring, like a small gear wheel moving an enormous gear wheel. He took Rue Democritus, thinking not of the atomic theory but of the speed limit, then Rue Newton, though his thoughts were far from the laws of motion and prisms and calculus; they were, rather, on the one-way signs. He turned down Rue Coulomb, reminding himself not of the attraction between electrical charges but that he had to buy a jack. After Rue Faraday he made a right onto Rue Maxwell, where it was not electromagnetic fields but his hunger that occupied him, and on Rue Einstein he accelerated, heedless of the theory of relativity. On Rues Planck, Rutherford, Schrödinger, and Pauli, the quantum theory did not cross his mind, or the atomic model, or wave mechanics, or electron spin. This thought, instead, as always: that the hangars, generators, and low office buildings with a few cars in front resembled Hollywood studios. The late afternoon sun, the mountain in the background, and the concentration on only one activity made a kind of Hollywood whose streets presented a topological equation he had to solve, block by block, to arrive as quickly as possible at the cafeteria, uncrowded at that hour.

He stands in line now, waiting his turn for dishes of assorted national origins, but dishes that have lost their character, speaking, instead, a tasteless culinary Esperanto. He chooses a domestic duck, domestic cheeses. A poke in his back, and a low voice: "Stay in line and pay without nodding to the cashier. Then you will receive further instructions."

Brahe smiles without turning, recognizes Rüdiger's voice. "What, are we going to an Arab emirate?"

They find an available table. Sitting, Rüdiger removes everything from his tray and arranges the plates geometrically before him: roast beef, spicy sauce, green vegetables separated by sections as in the plates of little children, Coca-Cola, flatware, paper napkin. Brahe, however, eats with his plate on the tray.

"So, how did it go with Wang?" Rüdiger asks.

"How did you find out about Wang?"

"I looked for you at home. Eileen told me about your appointment, the blueprint, and all the rest. She was proud of herself."

"She did an excellent job," Brahe says, chewing bread. "But Wang knew something was wrong." He tells his friend about the meeting in the hotel. But, telling the story, he realizes that the details are fading, the nuances, the expressions. Only the facts are left, so he concludes factually, "When Wang redoes his calculations, he will see that the change was no change at all."

"Is he really a shark?" asks Rüdiger, applying a thin layer of sauce to his meat.

Brahe leans forward. "At one point he looked at me as if to say: there is foul play here, and I'm not getting my twenty centimeters, but good for you for trying to fool me, I'm grateful that you took the trouble to try that. Then, on the stairs, he said that everything was moving too fast."

"Was it an escalator?" asked Rüdiger without looking at him.

Brahe smiles. "It was quicksand."

"Perhaps he's right, perhaps everything *is* moving too fast," Rüdiger says, taking vegetables from different sectors of his plate onto his fork. "Here we've only just started the experiment at Echenevex, have seen nothing yet, and are already thinking about what we will be seeing two years down the road."

"I'm in that experiment," Brahe says, cutting at the tiny duck with the tip of his knife.

"I am, too, but on the German team." Rüdiger smiles.

45

"I know, and I just gave you twenty centimeters."

"You mean, you just cheated me out of twenty centimeters."

Brahe pushes the rest of the duck aside, lowers his eyes. "I'm used to this pace, I can't imagine living differently. But I know that there is another kind of time, for emotion, which is out of sync with this time, and it seems to me that without emotion a thing is incomplete, that it won't be fixed in the mind, won't be remembered. It's been weeks since I've had a minute to myself, and I can't even remember the last time I went out with a woman. But that's not the point. I like this pace. This high-altitude flight from peak to peak without ever touching ground. Emotion, on the other hand, proceeds more slowly; it takes longer to start, longer to stop. Out of phase with events, it hovers near but never quite on, a kind of halo I am unable to perceive, and sometimes I have the impression that when I experience a thing, I remove it from its halo, and that therefore I won't be able to remember it later."

Rüdiger regards Brahe silently, stroking his mustache, straw-colored like his long hair, then says slowly, "You can forge the halo."

"Of course." Brahe sees, on the table, the orderly array of his friend's leftovers.

He looks up at an old woman with a raincoat and foulard behind Rüdiger. She stands, holding her tray, at the water dispenser. Behind her, a line of retired people visiting the installation. The old woman, holding her tray with both hands, positions her plastic cup beneath the spout, but now cannot decide which hand to use to press the faucet button. She looks at Brahe with a clumsy smile of distress. Rüdiger turns and says to her, "There's a pedal, on your left." She stares at the spout, then looks at the two men again, then again at the spout. "There . . . the pedal, use your foot." Rüdiger points and repeats "your foot" in all the languages he knows. Brahe gets up, goes around the woman, and presses the button for her. The water flows. She nods until the cup is filled.

The two men resume their conversation, though no longer on a specific subject. For a while they watch the line of old people heading for their tables, balancing their trays, struggling with the faucet button or the pedal. They are Belgian. They eat hurriedly, discussing, with exclamations, what they have seen that day. One of them asks Rüdiger, "Do you work here? Are you a scientist?"

Later, Brahe consults the Geneva phonebook. At E, he goes back and forth several times between Entemy and Eqwert before noticing the gap in the alphabetical sequence. He checks the directory's cover to see if it's the right year, then returns to the page and goes down the list of names with his finger, as if using Braille to find the missing name of Epstein.

On the way to Echenevex, the two men said nothing, each wrapped in his own thoughts, or watching the house lights here and there across the dark plain, the lights along the coast toward the mountains, the glow of the distant city reflected in the sky like a halo, the blinking red lights of the planes and on the antennas of the installation, the blue ground-lights of the airport runway. In the evening scene each light evoked a different feeling.

But in the long underground hall at Echenevex, the lights meant specific things. Some were shaped into numerals on indicators; some warned, said caution; some flashed in the form of explanatory pictures. This light did not serve as the background of an action but was the action itself; it did not illuminate the hand's movement but requested it, or answered it; it was not a contour, it was the content.

The button on Brahe's phone started to flash, indicating an outside call. Answering, he heard on the other end of the line a calm, slow voice. "Epstein." Followed by a moment of suspension.

"It is not easy," said Brahe, "to find your name in the phonebook."

"There's always something missing in directories. Are you taking photographs now?"

Brahe needed a moment to remember, then smiled. "I am."

"How are they coming out?"

"Quite well, I think."

"Can you prove that the children exist?" asked Epstein.

"Not yet. The children exist, of course. It's a merry-go-round, after all, as you called it. But one can't see them. At least not yet."

Another silence, in which Brahe looked at Rüdiger, who was at the end of the hall, climbing on the detector's scaffold among cables and railings.

"You haven't gone flying again?"

"No time."

"A shame you're so busy. You're underground?"

Brahe looked up at the concrete vault. "About a hundred meters. It's the deepest level, but it's quite comfortable. It's not a mine."

"If you ever have occasion to surface," said Epstein, "let's get together."

"Actually, I come up every day," Brahe said.

"Sundays too?"

"Oh yes. But when I'm up, I still have plenty to do."

"How about next Saturday? Come for breakfast. Our house is right on the lake. It's pleasant here."

"Okay," said Brahe. "Thank you."

"If any hitch develops, call me," said Epstein.

"Right, I'll use the number in the phonebook."

"Ah." Epstein laughed and a second later said, "Do you have pen and paper?"

5

They had finished eating and were full. Brahe was not surprised by the way Epstein touched objects: with precise calculation, with just pressure enough, raising the glass or knife, trusting the hand's natural force of attraction, to move them. Nor surprised by the perfect positioning of the pieces of furniture, so perfect that each seemed isolated against its white wall or glass door, isolated and yet interacting with all the other pieces of furniture, and with the plants, and with the soft lamps that at night would probably cast a light indistinguishable from the light of the day, so that even at midnight one would not know that it was late, an unusual, dramatic hour. Nor surprised by the cook-servant who emerged from the kitchen carrying and distributing with a sour, unspoken "Already?" at each course. Nor was Brahe surprised by Gilda, who had opened the gate for him, welcomed him, and said, "Mr. Epstein will be back in a minute. He is walking." Meaning, that the walking was not casual. Nor by Gilda's beauty, extraordinary, self-aware, so attuned to the things that exist between a woman and a man and take on new significance with each new experience. What surprised Brahe was the formality that Gilda and Epstein used with each other. A formality that excluded many possibilities but magnified others. Intense, unreserved, keeping no secrets. Or that was how it seemed to Brahe.

What surprised Gilda were Brahe's face, height, the clean cut of his eyebrows and mouth, the way he moved, which seemed to come not from an intellectual but an animallike perception of space. Especially this, that when Brahe spoke, his words remained on the surface, detached, impersonal, and strangely without weight. During the meal, she tried to guess the inner depth of that detachment. Her concentration drew little lines at the corners of her lips and dilated her azure irises, making them transparent.

Epstein, in turn, was surprised that a young man of science should be so curious about everything else, so carefully intent on joining all the parts to make a whole. To keep Brahe from drawing wrong conclusions, the writer had dropped such remarks in the conversation as, "Here, everything is rented, even the glasses," or, "Gilda works with me," or, "She's from the German part of Switzerland." Cuing Gilda, too, perhaps, on what to say and what not to say. She, for her part, followed Brahe down various lines of thought, and sometimes tried to guide him with small hints, as if to say, "No, not through here."

What surprised the cook was that, although the diners wanted to remain at the table as long as possible, the appetizer, first course, entree, vegetables, fruit, and dessert were all consumed with great speed. In no time, he had to pick up the plates, glasses, and leftovers. Clearing, he removed the tablecloth. Back in the kitchen, he took off his violet waiter's jacket, slipped into one of rough gray cloth, and went to work in the garden, not far from where Epstein and Brahe were sitting, at the rear of the villa, in the warm noon sun.

"How about a walk?" suggested Epstein, rising from his wicker chair.

"Good idea," said Brahe, though actually he wouldn't have minded remaining where he was.

Out of habit, Epstein takes the tile path, but cannot turn to speak to Brahe, who is right behind him, so he leaves the path, to walk side-by-side with his guest. He says, "There's space here, but little maneuverability. One foot off the tile, and you're trampling the lawn or disturbing the gravel border. You see the alder tree over there? I've been wanting to look at it up close, but I'm stopped by the thought of the footprints that would remain in the grass. The servant won't say anything, but he retaliates in small ways. He belongs to the house and I had to rent him along with it. At first, I wandered wherever I wanted, thinking that the grass would recover after a while, like all grass. I asked the servant, 'Why does it stay all shriveled up?' He said, 'It's not a carpet.' The next morning, wherever I had left a footprint, I found new tiles, new paths, connecting and branching, as if I had been allowed a more extensive route. All I had to do was take a few steps on the lawn and the next day there would be a walk there. Sometimes I feel I'd like to land somehow in the middle of the lawn, land flat with arms and legs outstretched, to leave him an imprint of my entire body, like the outline of a corpse, with no clue of how I got there or left. Or I'd just lie down, looking up at the sky. This is not a lawn; it's a film that records all human movement. Anyway, this area behind the house was finally, tacitly, given to me. Here I can walk at liberty, like an untameable animal."

They were walking back and forth slowly, on a long strip bordered by two hedges, where the grass had died completely. On one side was the house, on the other, the fence and the lake. Now and then Epstein would stop, silent, arms folded, eyes searching the surface of the water, the distant scene. Then he would approach the hedge, and at the hedge, talking, they would turn and face each other with that fraction of a miss that can make a swimmer lose a race. Brahe thought again of how Gilda spoke of Epstein walking. And he thought of the park, the afternoon sun, the lake; and that the garden that was off limits would be ideal to sit in. He said, "Is it so important that you walk?"

"Indeed," said Epstein. "It's more a question of internal rhythm. In my work, I have to walk. And in a way that's a shame, because when taking a walk one doesn't concentrate enough on walking; one is distracted mentally by the scenery, the conversation, as you and I are at this moment. Walking, one thinks, dictates, listens, observes—as if this continual loss of balance and regaining of balance were not important in itself. Have you ever thought how difficult it is to walk putting one leg in front of the other?"

"There are easier ways, I know," said Brahe. At the

hedge, instead of turning around, he turned for a moment to the right, the direction that would take him slowly, reflexively, irrevocably to the garden and the chairs.

"Of course there aren't." Epstein smiled, noticing Brahe's sidelong glance. "But if one pays attention, one realizes how the body, falling first to the left and then to the right to achieve one step, is governed by antagonism and alternation, but so quickly and smoothly that an intention or a direction is enough to make it all appear continuous."

For a while they were silent, each weighing the other's silence. Then Epstein said, "What do you see?"

"When?" asked Brahe. "In general, now, or at work?"

"Now. Tell me what you see now, at this moment. Close your eyes a second, then reopen them. Or keep them closed until the blackness seems perfect to you, without any image. Concentrate on the blackness, making it as black as you can. Then open your eyes and tell me what you see."

"Is there a prize?"

"No. Alas, you must consider your visual performance a completely uncompensated act."

Brahe purses his lips, puzzled. He looks at Epstein, at the garden, at the lake. Finally he closes his eyes, more out of courtesy than for any other reason. He reopens them almost immediately and, holding back a smile, says, "Where should I begin?"

"Wherever you like."

"With the garage?"

"The garage is perfect."

"The garage," Brahe enunciates carefully, then stops.

Epstein waits, then says, "And?"

"Well, there are the cars."

"What cars? What kind of cars?" prompts Epstein.

Brahe, changing his tone, recites patiently. "A white convertible Chevrolet, Geneva plates. A green Saab with a rear spoiler, Zurich plates. Then there's mine."

"Tell me, or don't you see it?"

"It's a Fiat 131, long, midnight blue, Geneva plates." Then he says, almost to himself, "The Saab appears to be in the best condition."

"Forget appearances. Tell me only what you see, only what is really there." He says this as a blind man speaking to one who sees. (And indeed, Epstein does not see the way Brahe sees.) He refrains from watching Brahe and what Brahe is observing; he keeps his eyes lowered on the automatic sprinkler in the middle of the garden. It spurts water, rotating slowly.

"A boat on the lake," says Brahe.

"A boat or a steamer or a motorboat or a Flying Dutchman?"

"A tourist boat," sighs Brahe, "with the outer deck under Plexiglas." He adds, "I don't know the manufacturer of the boat." Epstein nods yes, without moving his eyes from the sprinkler, as if "boat" will do.

Slowly, Brahe describes what he sees, without turning to see Epstein's reaction, though Epstein still has his face averted. Brahe follows no plan; he goes from one thing to another. Sometimes he begins "There is," other times he simply prefaces the noun with an "A" or a "Some." Plants, flowers, whose names he knows. When he doesn't know the names, he gives the color, or says "a medium-size tree." For the main veranda he says "what look like iron support beams" and "two deck chairs, benchlike, with long white cushions" and "a parabolic antenna, for satellite transmissions" and "two wicker chairs painted white." He sees "a tomahawk" in the portico; standing by the glass door at the entrance, he sees "light fixtures for evening" here and there in the lawn; he sees "a lawn mower without a motor" and describes the strip of cut grass up to the place where the mower stopped. Then he is silent.

"And people?" asks Epstein, eyes still on the sprinkler. "You see only objects, things. Is it possible there are no people? Where have you taken me?"

"This is your house."

"I'm only renting," says Epstein, smiling. And he turns for a second, but only for a second, to Brahe and says seriously, "There have to be people. Tell me what people you see." And resumes watching the water on the grass within the radius of the automatic sprinkler.

Epstein waits, but Brahe says nothing. Is it worth it, Epstein asks himself. Perhaps he should stop. With instinctive intolerance he wonders how a young man who is so curious can be unwilling to risk even a glance at people. Perhaps Epstein should say, "Come, that's enough." But the silence that follows will be disturbing, the forced change of subject will create a sense of failure, and it will be difficult to recapture the train of thought. Still, he is about to say, "Never mind." But Brahe, turning to observe the gardener, has already begun.

"A man in elegant trousers, wearing a jacket less elegant. He is leaning over a gentian." Then, as if that has broken the ice, he looks toward the garden through the half-open glass door. "A young woman with short blond hair and little makeup. She has a nice walk. She goes back and forth between a glass table and shelves filled with books." Then Gilda turns, and their eyes meet. A suspended moment. Brahe adds quietly, "She is looking our way."

Aware that the young man is now finished, has sat in a wicker chair, Epstein turns to him and asks, "And I?"

"You?" Brahe is surprised.

"Am I not here? You can't pretend not to see me, I'm too close. Unless I don't exist."

Various thoughts and feelings come to Brahe. The first, most obvious ones he gradually rejects, and with effort shifts his gaze to where he must look. The waiter-gardener seems closer now to the gentian, and Gilda closer to the glass door, with everything motionless and tense like Epstein's stare, which is waiting for him and which he finally meets. Brahe does not say, "There is a man," or, "A man," but, naturally, "You have white hair, slightly wavy. A lean face, gray eyes. You're wearing a plaid flannel shirt with the sleeves turned up to mid-forearm, a 1940s' chronometer on your wrist, a crocodile belt, trousers with cuffs and leather shoes flat like moccasins."

"Thank you," says Epstein, lowering his eyes.

A pause, while in the garden and in the house everything begins moving again, or so it seems to Brahe. Then Epstein says, "Now only you remain."

With a smile Brahe stretches his legs to the gravel, moves his feet inside his shoes. "I am me. I cannot see myself."

"I didn't mean to upset you," Epstein says after a while.

"I'm not upset," says Brahe.

"You have to admit you're peculiar. Asked to look, you see a Chevrolet, a boat, a tomahawk, a lawn mower. You see people only afterward, and then mainly their positions relative to things, or what they're wearing. But when you consider yourself, you are immediately aware of your inner reality. A strange dichotomy, isn't it?"

"Yes. How does it come about?"

"I don't know," says Epstein, his smile gone. "When one observes, one sees in physical terms; when one thinks, one thinks in terms nonphysical. But never both together. A man says, 'I am happy' or 'I am sad,' but he does not ask himself, 'Happy how? Sitting? Standing? In what position? Surrounded by what? Doing what? Touching what?' There's a woman with whom he is madly in love, or something for which he has such a profound nostalgia that he cannot even name it, or a friendship so strong that it seems unending, but while he takes cognizance of this, he does not take notice of the faucets he turns on, the handles he grips, the receiver he raises. He does not see the windows, banisters, doorknobs. He writes a letter, thinking about the person to whom it is addressed, not about the ink with which he writes it. All my work, throughout my life, has been to connect people to objects, and objects to experience, emotions, self-perception, ideas. Perhaps what I have created is nothing more than a lens that allows one to see the physical surroundings of one's inner life, giving both equal dignity. As a child you were perhaps drawn to mathematics, the sciences. I was drawn to people. I know them instinctively, with an animal sense. My *Atlas of Behavior,* the first book I wrote, mapped people in that way."

Epstein speaks with his chin resting on his hand. He is not using a particular tone, nor is he looking at any specific point, nor is he bothered that the servant is within earshot. Brahe, who has been listening while looking at the tops of his shoes, raising his eyes to the garden every now and then, by now realizes that Epstein can speak comfortably and directly about any person in that person's presence.

"Soon," Epstein continues, "I saw that I had another passion besides people: objects. I was able to feel how a thing was made, to feel its form in a way different from what is normally meant by perception. To feel, for example, what a filament feels in the vacuum of its pear-shaped bulb. It seems to me that every object had its own life—that it was not just a piece of matter worked into a shape, but also the thought behind it, the intention, the function. If someone designed the slant of a chair, it was as if the chair adjusted your back and arms, saying, 'Sit like this.' Or if someone made a light switch stiff enough for it to be turned on easily but not accidentally, the switch said to you, 'Your finger does not need to press so hard.' When I sat in the chair or turned the switch, and the current of its circuit went from its mind to mine, it did not matter that these things were all manufactured in quantity on assembly lines, I forgot the duplicates and heard one voice, as of a transmigrated soul, saying, 'I was built for you, only for you, for your hand alone, and for this story that you are writing now, so that you will understand how I am made.'

"In that way a relationship came to exist between me and others, many others, through things that appeared in the process of their being made, things that were much more than things. A kind of friendship was involved. Every object was behavior transformed into a thing, and then transformed back into behavior. This was how I worked. Basically with books one does more or less the same thing.

"In my books, if I told the story of a dwarf or a mother or a traveler, I would start from an umbrella, a sweater, the legs of a table. You may think of a visionary as one who sees marvels, or who sees a bridge straining to become an arch— not one who feels, without touching, the porosity of cement. I'm a visionary of what exists, of what is, and such vision can be just as disquieting for its precision and concreteness."

Brahe is all attention now, forgetting his discomfort. He follows Epstein's words, though his thoughts are going in three directions: in advance, to see where Epstein is heading; in retard, to reconstruct the course, lingering on the more familiar landmarks; and sideways, since it is enough to say dwarf, mother, or traveler to start the mind imagining.

Epstein is saying, "I learned to use objects, to run a boat, drive a car, pilot a plane. For each there were manuals, books seemingly intended more for the hand than for the heart, but I say seemingly, because I may have doubts about the purpose of the novels I have written but I know for certain that there is one and only one purpose of a manual: to increase the happiness of humanity. Manuals contain the names of things, describe their function, and tell what one should do for the enactment of that function. To me every manual was a book of etiquette, a novel on how to live. With each manual I learned a whole new nomenclature, a nomenclature that mapped onto the body, for each name corresponded to a movement, each movement to a feeling, a posture, a decorum, a perception, an insight. Each name was a possibility different from myself.

"It seemed to me that people's lives were linked to the lives of things. A human story, no matter what it was, would have in it chairs and beds, shoes and suitcases, tables and doors, automobiles, airplanes, trains, ships, drawers, boxes, things unnoticed in the background behind the people and thinking, 'Am I playing my part well?' Even in death. I once had to narrate a suicide. At the moment of maximum intensity, as the end approached, I made the character use what was closest to hand. I had him find a rope, inspect the ceiling, select a window, count pills, check the edges of razors or the caliber of the bullet in his revolver. I made him kneel before the gas stove and place his head where formerly he had placed the roast. I made him commit suicide, and yet I regarded that person as the blindest creature, for if in that instant he had seen the things he held in his hands, he would have renounced the act. But suicide is a sudden revenge of the ego, an inexplicable departure from the relationship between self and world."

Brahe uses Epstein's pauses to lean slightly forward, as if to obtain a better hold. Or his eyes steal to the garden. He knows that no answer is required, at least not yet, but still he fishes for another point of view, until Epstein resumes, this time in a more penetrating tone.

"Even memory . . . I'm at an age when a person should begin to understand what he has accomplished. I could ask myself what sort of man I was, astonish myself with the discovery that I was not at all what I thought I was when I was living second by second. I could brood on 'the past,' search it for meaning, for my continuity, the changes, the progress, and find nothing. . . . And yet there are areas of automatic, total recall, unexplored reserves you can tap in states of dozing. There you can feel, really feel, the squeak of skin on a balloon, the silkiness of a shock of hair, the roughness of a fabric, the pull of a steering wheel, the click of a lever between one's fingers. Only then do you understand how much you have aged. It is not in the lines of the face, the stoop of the body. Those are abstractions of age, like the rings (isobars on a weather map) in the trunk of a tree."

Epstein puts his hands in his pockets, crosses his legs. He meditates a little longer to himself, then says to Brahe, "Would you like a beer?"

"Yes, a beer," says Brahe. He looks at the servant, expecting him to be called over, but Epstein is already up, broad-shouldered, and heading for the house.

With the sudden responsiveness one experiences upon returning to a distant place or time, Brahe looks at the garden, the villa, for the girl in the studio, but she cannot be seen. Then, looking beyond the shore at the white Palais du Travail and the lake that narrows into the city's river, he calculates his exact position with respect to Echenevex. He feels far from the city, even though he is very close.

Epstein returns with a tray and two dark, slender bottles. With one hand he holds the bottles and with the other carefully removes the caps, not letting them fall. He pours beer in Brahe's glass, keeping down the foam, but leaves his own glass empty, drinking directly from the bottle. He wipes his mouth with a napkin and says, "Things are changing. Not in the common sense one gives to that sentiment. They are in fact disappearing. And the things arriving now, I'm afraid that I won't be able to feel them. That I'll only be able to use them."

"That bothers you?" Brahe glides a finger along the rim of his glass.

Epstein pulls his lower lip. "Not really. I never owned much. Even now I have only a Zlin, a Chevrolet, and a few thousand books. And I won't be around when those possessions disappear." He smiles. "Not that I'm nostalgic. Certainly planes and cars were a good way to feel time and remember it. But I don't think the past has value simply because it is the past. No, to be able to move on continually is praiseworthy. That's why I always hated collectors, that modest guild of time-defenders."

"Then what is it that occupies you?"

"Nothing occupies me. Actually, I'm very curious about this time of disappearing things. Perhaps, yes, I am bothered by the prospect of using without feeling. Friendship will be so much more difficult," says Epstein, turning to Brahe. "But there must be some connection between the disappearing of things and their visibility, because today I *see* my stories, I see them as never before. It's difficult for you to understand this and for me to explain. I used to see my stories while telling them, I would see them in the process of writing them. Now, I see them while looking, I see a story entirely from beginning to end simply by looking. And this," Epstein concludes on a tentative note, "is my experiment."

The water in the sprinkler suddenly collapsed. The waiter-gardener gathered up his tools, looked around quickly to see if he had forgotten anything, then went to the house. He came out a few minutes later in a different change of clothes, passed Brahe and Epstein with an impersonal raising and lowering of the hand, and, eyes straight ahead, took the brick path to the gate.

"You see him?" said Epstein.

"He doesn't sleep here?"

"No, thank goodness. He's not bad, really. The man could have been anything—except a waiter. A carpenter, a train conductor, anything but this. At Christmas I asked him, 'Aren't you taking a vacation?' He replied, 'Does nature take a vacation?' So I said, 'If it's because of the plants, just give me instructions.' He said, 'When I said nature, I was not referring to plants.' This house, you see, is maintained not by a servant but by nature itself in the form of a man."

They fell silent. Epstein looked at Brahe out of the corner of his eye. Amazed at the way the young man accepted whatever he was told, as if it were perfectly normal. He cleared his throat. "I told you that seeing stories is my current experiment. Perhaps I should explain."

Slowly, Brahe said, "No need. I understood."

Gilda came out into the garden and sat in front of them. She was wearing slacks, short at the ankles, and a jacket that accentuated her shoulders. To Epstein she said, "I checked the notebooks. You were right, Ira. I left everything on the table." He nodded. She pulled her feet up onto the chair, hugged her legs, and with her chin resting on her knees watched the two men. As though she knew everything that they had told each other. The irises of her eyes were all one color, without flecks, which made them deeper, more slate blue than sky blue; they seemed to absorb and concentrate the light of day. Brahe was so drawn to them that he had to exclude them from his field of vision. Like looking at the lines on a sheet of music but not the notes.

They spoke about Geneva, Italy. About Germany, to which country Epstein had not returned for many years ("I'm getting closer by stages," he said). About Gilda, who came from Zurich but stayed here for long periods to work with Epstein. She had a room in the villa, because sometimes they would work until late at night, but usually she returned by midafternoon to Geneva, where she had a small apartment. They talked about Brahe's work, but he said that the ring, about thirty kilometers wide, had only just been completed, and his was one of the first experiments. Talking, they knew that what they said was unimportant compared to the intimacy that grew beneath the conversation, as little by little the light dimmed over the lake and city, and puffs of the whitest clouds hung in the red sky.

Then Brahe said, "I have to go." He tried to say good-bye to Gilda in a way completely neutral, but it ended up too hurried and brusque, or so he thought.

Hands in his pockets, Epstein walked him to the car. When Brahe was seated, Epstein said, holding the door, "Did you know that Einstein taught in Prague in 1911 and 1912?"

"I knew he'd been there," said Brahe.

"Franz Kafka was there also. In Prague."

Brahe, his feet on the pedals, felt awkward. He was tempted to say, "Einstein is Einstein, but Franz Kafka?" Instead, he smiled. "Well, Prague was his city."

"Do you think they ever met?"

"I don't know. Prague is large; it must have been large even then."

Epstein moved gravel with his shoe. "It's unthinkable that they never met. After all, they both had to contend with the Law."

"Perhaps they moved in different circles," said Brahe, turning the key.

"Don't you think that in those two years they might at least have bumped into one another in the street? Even if they didn't know one another, they might have exchanged glances. It's impossible that two men like that should not have felt each other's presence."

Brahe gripped the wheel and said, "Who knows? Perhaps they met but thought it best not to let the world know."

"Or they met," said Epstein, casting an eye around the garden, "in a parallel time. Perhaps there are times parallel to ours in which Einstein and Kafka leave their houses every day and meet, or almost meet, turning around at the last moment and returning home. Or cyclical times in which Einstein and Kafka meet every few years and say, 'You again!' Or confused times in which they expect to meet, to meet momentarily, but never do, because in reality they already met, though neither was aware of it. Or bifurcated times in which they meet and don't meet at the same time, and the meeting and the nonmeeting are totally equivalent."

Brahe said, "Time goes in one direction, only one."

"But haven't you demonstrated precisely that that is not so? That time can go backward?"

"Yes, with the collision of two particles. With three, that

66

becomes highly unlikely. With four, the probability of time moving backward is so minute that it borders on the impossible. Mr. Einstein and Mr. Kafka, together, comprise billions and billions of particles in continual transformation and flux. Not even their combined genius could make them go backward in time." Brahe regarded Epstein with great seriousness. "The Law is splendid. Imagination, too, is splendid. But in an experiment, unfortunately, only what can be proved has value." And he said this with a sorrow that surprised them both.

"I know," said Epstein, lowering his eyes. He smiled and closed the door.

Brahe started the car, put an arm on the back of the seat next to him as if there were a person's shoulders there, and turned around as he put the car in reverse. He left the villa accelerating, swaying on the wheel suspensions.

6

I should have been more explicit with him. But how? How can I explain that I see stories? Not fragments, images, ideas, but whole, completed stories that begin when I look and end when I stop looking, without the need of a single word. How can I explain this to anyone else? I could tell it in a novel, but that would be turning back. Perhaps in a daily report, a journal, a lab book in which I describe the experiment. But can I call an experiment what happens when I see a black limousine with a little flag on the hood, and another black limousine without the flag, and two station wagons carrying rigid men with short haircuts, and all these cars are directed toward disarmament and global peace, and even before the procession has turned the corner my story is finished? How can I call an experiment a thing that is not reproducible by others under the same conditions, even though no conditions are ever exactly the same? And why should another accept the rules I set myself at the beginning, rules that (as I gradually discovered) are nothing but the form of what happens, the facts of my situation? How to explain that each story is born only in what I see, not in my memory? That it has to be rigorously brought to an end, not left for another to end, and tested and retested, all during the seeing? And the time of the seeing, how long is it? How does the external time correspond to the time, internal, of my vision, which is determined by the story itself? I could have said to him, "You see, it's like a fuse blowing, it's as if I opened a door intending to enter and instead I exited. Do you understand, feel that?" I could have said to him, "It's strange that here you are trying to see things, when things are disappearing." Don't you understand that these things coming into existence are pure energy, pure light, pure imagination, not things at all, but *nonthings*? That they do not require the contact of our bodies, only our feelings? Not the hand any longer, but the heart, the mind? That they are lines of energy intertwined with our lines of energy, trajectories without objects trajected? And don't you wonder what happens when the imagination outside meets the imagination inside, or, better, when outside and inside no longer exist and there is only one uninterrupted circuit of imagination? I am one who tells stories, who always told stories, until now, until this new set of circumstances, when I began to see them born full-grown, and this is my experiment. Don't you feel that everything is much lighter, that it's velocity without mass? Aren't you curious about the feel of this? A pity I can't describe it. There is something amoral in not being able to describe, just as there is something highly moral about a good description. Not needing to describe is the only thing that jeopardizes the happiness of seeing beyond form.

These were Epstein's thoughts after Brahe left his house.

7

"And what was the woman like?" Rüdiger asked as they entered central stores, the project's stockroom.

"Pretty," said Brahe. He nodded to a man in a blue coat behind the counter, who was talking to another man in a blue coat behind the counter.

"Pretty, how?" Rüdiger asked.

"Very pretty."

"Yes, but could you be more specific?"

"In what way?" Brahe began to look carefully among the shelves.

"A detail or two beyond her name."

Brahe turned to Rüdiger with a smile. "We have shopping to do, don't we?"

Rüdiger nodded and took a list from his shirt pocket. Morning light, filtering down through little windows near the ceiling, mixes with the smell of rubber, plastic, and metal.

They proceeded between shelves that held parts for vacuum lines, insulated pipes, joints of various types, manifolds, couplers, gas barriers, cryogenic valves. They passed a large selection of shields for the focusing and curving magnets, and shelves containing potentiometers, klystrons, and the niobium plates for the superconducting. They did not stop to look at any of this, since none of it was of use to the detectors. It was not directly involved with the seeing, only with the preparation for the seeing. Then, the shelves containing scintillation counters, light-cables, photomultipliers arranged according to type and power, photodiodes, phototriodes, all of the highest resolution.

Brahe and Rüdiger stopped in the computer section, the heart of the seeing process. Here, banks of diskettes: software. Programs for file processing, for filtering and analyzing background noise, for memory storage, recall, piggybacking, and parking. Diskettes for ultrafast compiling-assembling-translating, for language processing to enable the instruments to speak, for widening the windows of observation by precious nanoseconds and picoseconds, since what was seen had a duration unimaginably infinitesimal, and only through computer reconstruction from microscopic traces could one tell—with rigor, with proof—what had been generated before it transformed itself immediately into something completely different.

Brahe looked up at the stockroom walls: rolls of silicone tape, coolants, coils, motors with direct and alternating current, keyboards, monitors, imagers, optical fibers, feeders, galvanometers, Geiger counters for safety, endoscopes to inspect inaccessible places, and plastic buckets, sponges, and scrub pads.

"A lot of stuff," Rüdiger said, fingering a diskette.

71

Each item is displayed with equal dignity. The machines, their parts, and their software are all here, each with its own catalog number. In order, available, like a vocabulary.

One by one, Brahe went through the drawers of a metal chest, shallow, like those for illustrations; he was looking for multiple connectors. He took some out, held them to the light, put them back. He asked, without looking up, "You don't remember the number, do you?"

Rüdiger, too, rummaged in the drawers. "No, but we'll find it."

They examined the connectors. Rüdiger ran a thumb over the jacks and the plugs, counting them that way. Brahe stopped looking, got up, stepped back, watched Rüdiger. Incredible, the man's ability to apply himself to anything with the same quiet intensity, the same surprise and pleasure, without any prioritization of time. Admiring, Brahe thought, "Nothing can distract him, for everything is equally important. Distraction does not exist for him."

Brahe went over to spools of cables hanging on a display stand, which he turned slowly, looking idly at the multicolored strips, then returned to the chest of drawers where Rüdiger still knelt. Taking a jack with a double letter printed on the side, one uppercase, one lowercase, Brahe said, "Here." Rüdiger looked at the jack, then at Brahe, and smiled.

At the cashier's desk, Rüdiger gave the man in the blue coat the price tags, and Brahe produced his I.D. Everything went into the ledger with a push of a button; the items were charged to the budget of their experiment.

At the entrance they stopped by a shelf marked "Obsolete. Take what you want." Rüdiger asked, "Shall we have a look here, too?"

Brahe thought a second, then shook his head. "No, better not." But sometimes on the junk table he found parts for equipment he was still using, or even the same parts he had just bought and paid for at the counter.

They left central stores and drove back to Echenevex in Rüdiger's car. Brahe watched the scenery moving past the dashboard. Rüdiger kept both hands on the wheel. "What if we see nothing?" he said. This, a coda to his thoughts, without anxiety.

"That's possible," Brahe said. The sun was strong, a summer sun. He looked at the yellow of the fields, the dark outline of the Jura mountains, the gray lines of the installations. It was that time of the year, now, when in the evening, as he parked in front of the hangar before going underground, there was still some light, a scent of grass, a quality to the air that did not belong at all to the work feeling.

"And if others see something before we do?" Rüdiger went on in the same tone.

"In that case, many possibilities will open up for you. A teaching position in some university. American offers. Or you could get a good job at Telefunken."

"Where Isadora Duncan worked?"

"There, you see? A place with a great tradition."

Rüdiger put a hand out the window, signaling a turn. "And how about you? Would you go to America?"

"I don't know. I don't think so. Europe interests me." They arrived at a huge beige-and-blue hangar surrounded by rows of beech trees and green underbrush. "In any case, we still have time. Sooner or later, we'll see something."

Entering the driveway, they saw a fire truck on the grass, with a fireman standing on the running board.

"Oh no," said Rüdiger.

"Wednesday, again: exit drill."

"Who's down there now?"

"Maybe Mark, if he stayed late," Brahe said.

They passed the automatic security gate, took the elevator, and entered the underground hall, clipping their radiation badges on their jackets. Mark, a venerable British physicist, was arguing with the fire chief and two other men in uniform at the base of the detector. "But it's totally pointless," he was saying. "I was up the stairs last week." He wore an electric-blue tie over a red plaid shirt; gray trousers; sandals with socks. "Poor Mark," said Rüdiger, putting the shopping bag on the table.

The old man argued without real conviction, and the fire chief listened to him with folded arms, kind and patient, as if they were both participants in a small, unavoidable ceremony. Finally Mark turned to Brahe and said, "Pietro, explain to him. He thinks I'm not working because the beam's not on." Brahe had promised himself not to argue again with the firemen, so he merely shrugged. The chief said, "Just show us that you know where the emergency equipment is, and the procedure. We'll go up only partway, then you can come down again."

The old man sighed. The chief turned to Brahe and Rüdiger: "And you? Aren't you coming?"

"No," said Rüdiger. "We work at night. This is not our shift." The chief stood for a moment, looking at them dubiously. Then he accompanied Mark to the end of the hall. As they passed under the yellow blinkers, Mark pointed out, one by one, the switches that he would have to throw, the cabinets that he would have to open, the things he would have to take out, and how to use them in case of fire. He described the steps rather than walk through them, not wanting to waste time.

Then the group could be seen appearing and disappearing on the blue stairs between the floors. The old man was still arguing with the firemen. But finally they let him go back downstairs.

When he entered the hall again, his face wore a completely different expression: quick, self-confident. "I thought you were asleep," he said to Brahe. "Otherwise I would have called you. The transmission stopped at ten. I think we have something."

"What?" asked Brahe, tense.

"Hard to tell. The pictures are still unclear. But you can see something. The numbers, at least, show something."

"A candidate?" said Rüdiger.

"Well, 'candidate' is a big word," said the old man, sitting at the keyboard. "But there was definitely an event, around seven, about an hour after you left."

They were in one of those white-paneled semi-interiors used even within this huge concrete tunnel for partitioning space and movement, for concentrating light—in short, for making a "home." A custom that always amazed Brahe. He and Rüdiger looked over the old man's shoulders, waiting for the data to be retrieved from the memory. Mark's hair was all white. He was "prewar," belonging to an earlier generation. Brahe remembered the first time he saw Mark. Brahe was still a student then, and the physicist had agreed one night to demonstrate his *forte*: computing integrals without writing them down, in his head. People in the audience gave the problems, he would touch his eyes for a minute, then write the answers on the blackboard. Afterward, Brahe introduced himself and asked him about his system. Mark replied, "I don't actually do a calculation. There isn't time. I let the numbers do it. Numbers lead to numbers by themselves. One has to feel it."

So at the opposite end of the scale from the sharks were men like Mark, the scientists of passion. "Maybe my problem is," Brahe thought, "that I'm only half shark, and the other half is like Mark."

"No visualization?" asked Rüdiger.

"No, only figures." Mark pointed at the numbers now descending in rapid columns.

The three men looked at the green screen, concentrating on the numbers, trying to picture what happened, for each number signified an energy, an amplitude, a direction, each was a circle or line or an ellipse forming or an angle of incidence or a unit of time. Each told of the symmetries of time and space, of the play of variables and constants, of the continual alternation between wave and particle, between one name and another name, and of the Law that allows to happen all that can happen, forbidding only what cannot.

They were silent, expectant, their minds extrapolating,

predicting, then rushing back to the numbers, then making the trip again, with less haste, gradually discovering what was missing, like a man entering his house after a burglary.

"What do you think?" Mark asked.

"Here it opens well, but closes immediately," Rüdiger said.

"But it increases here, see?"

"Yes, but doesn't peak." Then Rüdiger gave Brahe a sidelong glance. "And you, Pietro, what do you think?"

"Here, it's too low. Here, too short," Brahe said, pointing. He looked at Mark, who had an arm over the back of his chair, the electric-blue tie dangling. And at Rüdiger, who was hunched over the console waiting for an answer. Then Brahe stopped thinking about the numbers, certain now that there was nothing to see, and instead asked himself if he would remember this. He thought how different they all were from one another, though joined by circumstances, and that their friendship could exist only here, this moment, and nowhere else. He smiled and said, "Not conclusive. But it's a beginning."

"And, for today, nothing?" asked Rüdiger.

"Nothing," said Brahe, touching his eyebrow.

Rüdiger took one of the new diskettes from the table, inserted it in the drive, and punched keys, while Brahe and Mark went over the printout.

Before leaving, Brahe took one last look at the detector at the end of the hall. Once, when the machine was still being built and had not yet been connected to the ring, he entered the tunnel and walked five hundred meters in one direction, then in the other. It was smaller than a subway tunnel, neon-lighted, and at its center was the acceleration tube. Amusing, to think of going home by entering here and exiting at Ferney-Voltaire, as if it were a station six or seven kilometers to the east. He looked at the scaffolding, the cables surrounding the experiment. They called the detector the experiment, combining in one name the machine and its purpose, the thing determining and the thing determined. Later, as they followed Mark's old Jaguar to the cafeteria at the installation, Rüdiger said, slumped in his seat, "I'm tired, yes, but I don't feel sleepy."

"You should try to sleep, at least a little. Otherwise, tonight will be a disaster," Brahe said. He drove slowly, eyes on the road and on Mark's head, which was visible through the Jaguar's rear window.

"Perhaps," Rüdiger reflected, "one begins life with x amount of sleep, which is gradually consumed, and when it's exhausted, one needs no more. Or x amount of kilometers that one can do on foot. Or x amount of seafood. Or x amount of excitement, which diminishes until there is no more."

Brahe smiled. "And x amount of women?"

Rüdiger grunted, stroked his blond mustache. "Let's hope that that supply has not been used up."

"Look, fallow deer," Brahe said, slowing down, crossing to the opposite shoulder of the road, almost touching the fence. It was not easy to see the deer. The instant they heard a car, they vanished into the foliage, but after a while reappeared with their moist eyes and muzzles. Brahe always felt uneasy confronting the purity of these animals—true animals, not pets. As if they were more moral than he. At the same time he found it incomprehensible that one could be, could want to be, different from them, separate from them. Epstein had said something on this subject the first time they met; Brahe tried to remember what, but couldn't because Epstein's ideas, once they surfaced, spread in multiple lines to form a continuum in which one thought merged with another. Mark, who also had stopped, began to back up, so Brahe put the car back into gear and said, "Let's go."

In the cafeteria, people stopped from time to time at their table, entering and leaving the conversation with light smiles, brief greetings, a quick question about the situation in Echenevex. Having finished eating, Brahe urged Rüdiger to get some sleep that afternoon and asked Mark to drive him home. Brahe said he would pick Rüdiger up in the evening. Then he headed for Ferney-Voltaire, took the underpass under the airport runway, went through the countryside—but at a gas station turned around (while the attendant was getting up from his chair) and went back to Geneva. He parked on one of the large boulevards near the bridge.

An uncrowded sidewalk. More pedestrians near the store windows, which displayed sport jackets, hunting jackets with many pockets, suggestive of adventure, of journeys that no one took anymore. And suits with narrow collars: for the urban environment, where every encounter was controlled and predictable, governed by glances, gestures, clothes, by allusions and references and not the things themselves. Reducing adventure to measured costumes, to little mise-en-scenes.

In an international bookstore he asked a clerk for

assistance, unaccustomed to counters and shelves. He found it strange that there were books on everything, everything except his field, and the few that were were general, superficial. The things that concerned him vitally were compared to orange segments, club sandwiches, tennis balls, cars on trips of billions of kilometers, snails, bullets, glasses of water, and football fields. The invitation was usually, "Imagine a . . . ," and he would be told to consider something totally different from the object of his research. The world had been changing for more than half a century, yet an extraordinary conservatism of the imagination and perception ignored that change, retreating to the past. It was necessary, of course, to explain. But how could he explain that for what he was trying to see no metaphor existed, no image, only the clichés of popular science, which made science an alphabetical picture book for children?

He asked at the desk, "Do you have a novel by Ira Epstein?"

The clerk said, "Which one?," and Brahe realized that he did not know any of the titles.

He was led to a shelf that contained all of Epstein in various languages, colors, and sizes. Odd, that the same story should come in so many different covers. Brahe looked at the various photographs of the author on the flaps. Book by book, Epstein's way of dressing became freer. First the jacket went, then the tie. The shirt collar opened. Even the face grew less formal. More detached, ironic, sunny.

Brahe bought two books. On his way back to the car he read the flaps, which told him exactly where Ira Epstein was born and when. The biographical notes were minimal, however, because of the space taken up by the long list of his books, but Brahe tried to fill in what had been left out.

With the books on the passenger's seat, he opened to a page at each traffic light, any page, and read until the cars behind him politely tapped their horns. In this way he arrived at the border and crossed to the little town of Ferney, passing Castle Voltaire, closed as always, slanted sunlight on its gray roofs.

Neither Eileen nor Sarad was at home. Brahe thought of the Indian, who was building a machine to catch the faint gravitational waves that resulted from the explosion of stars or their collision, and he thought of the English girl who designed magnets, and a nostalgia came over him: for the slow time of preparation, so different from this urgent time of the experiment in which he now lived, this tension that neither success nor failure would relieve.

He went upstairs, put the books on his desk, and took a long shower.

Later he began to read one of the novels, following the plot and characters in a language not his own, which made each word stand out almost like Braille. He tried to hear, in the writing, Epstein's voice, and thought he found it.

Highly precise descriptions of things, of the relationships between events and emotions. Details that made him think, "Yes, life is like that." Looking up from the book at the objects in his room, he retained the perspective of the characters and also of the narrator, a perspective that gave a dignity even to his lying on the bed in his trousers and bare-chested. From time to time he came upon sentences, especially at the end of paragraphs, which like nets collected all that went before them, and these could be hauled to shore, detached from the story, and taken away. One such sentence: "He knew that he could no longer lie down among words as an animal in its den."

8

"How about a drink in the city?" suggested Epstein, rising from his desk.

Gilda looked up from the pages in front of her. "In a sophisticated place?"

"Very sophisticated."

On some days their work ended this way, suddenly. Days, for example, in which Gilda would raise an important question; when Epstein, after a silence, would say, "Let's go to the city, but you drive," meaning that they were calling it quits. Depending on the hour, they would either go to lunch or out for a drink, or just drive into the city together if Gilda had a prior engagement, then Epstein would return on foot to Bellerive.

When Gilda came downstairs from her room, having changed, Epstein was struck once again by the ease with which she went from woman to girl or girl to woman. It was in the way she absorbed the light. One of her most attractive qualities. He opened the car door for her and said, "Mind if we take mine? Then I'll leave it with you."

"Fine. But why?"

"We have an appointment with Doctor Brahe and one of his friends."

Now they follow the edge of the lake, not hurrying, with the top down. They move ahead in a large vista that includes their profiles and the modern part of the city, and the quays on both shores connected by a line of boats. Epstein looks at large buildings with flags and many windows. Behind those windows a northern, temperate bureaucracy works for a peaceful solution to the wars and massacres of tropical countries. The light itself bespeaks neutrality: not sunny, not gray, but a bright summer afternoon. It is difficult, Epstein thinks, for this city to have a character of its own. All other cities have some focal point, a feature to which their guests must conform, but a city dedicated to indiscriminate hospitality, how can it have character? Neutrality means no temperament; one cannot expect passion from an international organization. But Epstein himself is not unlike the host organizations residing in Geneva, being a temporary resident; and perhaps he too is here for purposes, albeit personal, of negotiation.

"There they are!" said Gilda, pointing to Brahe and Rüdiger, who were standing on the shore front. Epstein drew up to the curb and parked. He and Gilda got out, and there were introductions and smiles. Rüdiger gave the full German-style greeting, clicking his heels and bowing repeatedly as he shook Epstein's hand and brushed Gilda's with his lips. Epstein caught the amused eyes of Brahe, who was shaking his head. Brahe, for his part, felt Gilda's eyes on himself, and tried to meet them, but instead looked at the gardenia in her lapel. Gilda, noticing this, wondered if something was wrong with the flower. There was a moment of adoration involving Rüdiger and the Chevrolet: he circled the old convertible, examined the tires, the paint, the trim, and finally congratulated Epstein, who really didn't care much about the car.

They drove to the old city. Epstein slid the nose of the car down narrow, stone-paved streets, around hairpin curves that made the tires squeal even though he was going slowly. From time to time Gilda turned around to Brahe and Rüdiger in the back seat. When she spoke or smiled, Brahe could see her perfectly round cheekbones, the clean-cut outline of her eyelids, the contour of her lips, the curve of her ear, around which her short hair curled, and he thought that if she was so beautiful at that distance, her beauty would be unbearable closer up, where one would have to shut one eye to see. Rüdiger held the back of Epstein's seat, as if wanting to push him, and at one point said, "But can this kind of car go fast?" Epstein smiled at him in the rear-view mirror. "Of course it can, but not here."

They parked on an uphill street, then continued on foot between small gray and beige buildings, and the difference in color was the only boundary between one house and the next. All had sloping roofs, added-on skylights, spires. The street names and memorial plaques on doors told of a city of religious schisms, of infighting, debates, and treachery. A strange contrast, thought Epstein: down there, the modern city was completely neutral and nonpartisan, up here, the old city was fiercely, totally partisan.

Epstein and Brahe walked considerably behind Gilda and

Rüdiger. The four divided after having tried unsuccessfully, awkwardly, to proceed all abreast on the narrow sidewalk. Rüdiger, in his orange-plaid jacket, made large circular motions with his arms; Gilda, head bent slightly, listened attentively.

"Do you think he is telling her about high-energy physics?" asked Epstein.

"No doubt," smiled Brahe.

They ascended past little antique shops, shops that sold only a few items, or even only one item, as if there were a market for them: walking sticks, clocks with pendulums, snuffboxes, old suitcases. Epstein always felt perplexed by this kind of store, where objects outlived their users, were abstracted from their use, bereft of feelings, orientation, and balance. Things dead but unburied.

"And how is it going, your work?" asked Epstein.

"How is yours?" Brahe said, looking at Gilda, who was tall and thin in her slacks and light linen jacket. Elegant, unattainable.

"I asked first."

Brahe brushed his eyebrow. "We're not seeing much, but it's much more than he thinks." And he pointed gently at Rüdiger, who from time to time stopped, gesticulated, then continued walking, holding Gilda's elbow.

"Why don't you tell him?"

"It's not a matter, really, of telling him or not telling him. I contain the enthusiasm so the disappointment won't be too great."

"Is that difficult?"

"No, but one part of you runs ahead; it projects what it wants to see, then it believes that it is seeing that. And there's another part which holds back constantly. It says: Let's go back, let's recheck. It's like a slower leg. You drag it after you, yet put more weight on it."

"I understand," Epstein said.

They were silent a while, then Brahe spoke. "And your work?" Trying to put the question in a neutral, casual tone.

"In my work, as I already told you, one sees a great deal. So much, sometimes, that little is left for the imagination." He ran a hand through his white hair. "But that is only a point of departure."

Before a hardware store that looked like a boutique, Epstein stopped for a second. He loved hardware stores: in the window, the drills, electric saws, different screwdrivers and wrenches arranged according to size represented a dictionary of all that could be done. And it seemed to him that each year the handles were becoming more colorful, that there was less iron in the tools. He liked the idea of useful things being as light and colorful as shoes and clothes. This way, everything appeared less important. Even ideas, he thought, are becoming lighter, more colorful, less important.

When they caught up with Gilda and Rüdiger at the corner, she turned and looked at Brahe so suddenly and so deeply that he could not avert his eyes and had to hold his breath. Epstein, noticing, said with a smile, "Have you picked out a place where we can have our drink?" Rüdiger pointed to a bar that, because of its wrought-iron sign, looked little different from the antique shops on the square. They entered a place that was half pub, half cafeteria. Young couples sat in booths bent over tall tropical drinks that they sipped through curved straws.

Rüdiger chose a dark beer from a long list. They sat at a corner table, where music and voices gathered in an almost palpable density. The conversation drew in all four, but then gradually a kind of centrifugal force was created, where each found himself pushed to the limit of what he was saying, more and more distant from the center, at which it is natural to think one thing and simultaneously entertain the possibility of its opposite. And sometimes the conversation split into twos and took on a more intimate tone. Gilda asked Brahe:

"Have you visited Voltaire's Castle?"

"No."

"Don't you live in Ferney?"

"Yes, right by the castle. But it's closed all year, except for a few days in August, and even then one can visit it only at certain hours."

"Like a natural phenomenon?" said Gilda with a sudden transparency in her blue eyes.

"Yes." Brahe smiled.

"Is it beautiful?"

"It's not really a castle. It's a large villa with a gray roof and a garden."

In conversation Gilda seemed remarkably pliable. She followed him from subject to subject, not questioning his sudden changes of direction; she anticipated him silently, was there waiting for him at the crucial points, like a person who walks beside you but suddenly appears up ahead. Perhaps this was because Brahe was able now to remain entangled in her eyes, without seeking safety in the lines of her lips or ears. Finally she looked above him and said, "Have you seen the fish behind you?"

Brahe turned. He was so tall, his head brushed the print hanging on the wall. Then he noticed that there was another print in the corner, and others, too, of different fish, all hung at the same height, like a line floating over the people seated at the tables.

"What kind of fish are they?" Gilda asked.

"Are there titles underneath?" Rüdiger asked.

Brahe smiled at him—titles of fish?—but looked closer. The scientific names in italics on the nearest prints did not tell him much. Epstein was silent, comparing the fish. In the one behind Brahe, the yellow dots might have been scales or reflected light; another fish, though, had bright papillae at the ends of the long rays of its fins, like broken optic fibers; on the mouth of a third there was a tube-shaped protuberance that curved and ended in a little lamp.

"I don't know about those over there," said Epstein, "but these are all lantern fish."

They speculated a while, agreeing that the fish could not be from Lake Geneva, since lantern fish inhabited the deep sea. The phenomenon was chemiluminescence, a cold light, according to Brahe, who once studied animal electricity. But then how could the draftsman, an eighteenth-century naturalist, have drawn the fish with their lights on, since he must have seen them only dead, with their lights off? Or had he imagined the light, reproducing it in such a natural way that they themselves had not questioned it at first?

"But I don't think that the light goes off immediately,"

said Gilda. Then added thoughtfully, "One night I went fishing with a friend, and the first thing he caught was something between a plant and a fish. It had no precise shape, but under its eyes was a glowing bulb. This bulb was always on; the fish, unable to turn it off, could only cover it with a membrane or rotate it inward. I wanted to look at it better, but my friend tore out the bulb, as you would remove a pea from its pod. 'Why?' I screamed, and he replied that he needed it as bait to attract normal fish, and that he had to pull it out immediately, because this fish, as a last resort before dying, would swallow the bulb. 'It swallows its own light,' he said."

Epstein stared at the print, speechless. Rüdiger said, "Well . . ." And Brahe thought: the first time you meet a woman, she tells you something that she did with her friend.

There were moments when the voices in the bar lowered, an ebb in the wave that allowed their voices to emerge. Then they would hurriedly conclude their sentences, muffle them, and join the general silence. In one of these ebbs, Brahe looked at his watch, calculated the time needed to return to Echenevex, and said, "We have to go."

On their way to the car, they divided as they had before, but this time Epstein and Brahe went first. They walked down the same narrow streets, talking but now without the anxiety to fill the occasional silences between them, as if a certain stability made these silences natural, allowing the possibility of being together but also apart. At a turn, Brahe looked at the lake and the mountains: the inclined lines of the slopes, the horizontal of the surface of the water. He looked at them as if from the sky and said, "Here is a thing that has disappeared: the seaplane."

"Yes, they were beautiful," said Epstein. "There still are some around the world, mostly in countries where there are long rivers or many lakes. Some in Africa, some in South America. They originated in Europe, but are rarely seen here nowadays."

"Those were small," said Brahe.

"Small or medium-size. Often they were regular planes with a pair of floats attached."

"Actually, I was thinking of the big seaplanes, with one central hull, high wings, and several engines."

Epstein looked at Brahe with amusement. "You mean the Shorts, the Latécoères, the Blohm und Vosses?"

"And the Macchi," said Brahe, also smiling.

"The Macchi, of course." Epstein went on: "They were all very strange. When they landed, they immerged halfway up the nose, like a hippopotamus in a river. When they lifted off, they produced a waterfall. Making it seem that the essence of water lay not in the wetness but in the sliding away and flowing."

Epstein, hands in his pockets, turned to look at Gilda and Rüdiger, but they were not in sight. He said, "Inside, they had doors with the threshold raised, watertight doors as in ships. Many had two decks, with interior stairs. There were berths for the night, so if you wanted, it was possible to land and sleep on the water, then take off at dawn. Some, the biggest, even had a dining room."

"Like Howard Hughes's?" said Brahe.

"His was the biggest, a seaplane that carried seven hundred passengers, an immense pearl-gray fish. Never before had such a plane been built. All the parts were brought to Terminal

Island: wings, rudder, ailerons, flaps, the eight three-thousand-horsepower engines. To carry the hull down the street, they had to move back telephone poles and street lights and cut down trees. It took an entire year to assemble. Then one morning in front of a thousand people on the quay, almost all of Hollywood, Howard Hughes sat down at the controls, started the engines, let the plane taxi, then turned it off. A half an hour later, he started up again and flew a short distance over the water, as if he were a transatlantic pilot. Then another wait. After all, he was a showman. Finally he started the engines again, made another short flight, about a mile, landed, and quietly returned to the quay. The seaplane is still there; it never flew again."

They reached the car. Epstein turned and looked down the street. "Do you think Gilda and your friend are coming?" he asked Brahe with a smile, as if asking him to choose what should happen.

"Yes, I think so," said Brahe.

They sat in the Chevrolet with the top down. Everything in the piazza seemed too carefully arranged, like pure white marble unrelieved by a single crack. Epstein said, "Yes, Hughes had the biggest. But there was another giant: the Short-Mayo Composite, a massive British seaplane that carried on its back a second, smaller seaplane to be launched in flight. The idea was that the lower plane would consume more of the fuel, permitting the upper one to take off in midair with its tanks almost full and thereby increasing its range. The upper plane was not that small: a four-engine Mercury for the mail service, with no central hull but two floats and very streamlined. They would take off with their eight engines synchronized, then the mail plane would be released and the Short-Mayo would return. This way, the Mercury could go from Scotland to Alexander Bay at the mouth of the Orange River in South Africa without stopping to refuel. That was at the end of the thirties. The war divided the two seaplanes. The Short-Mayo was used for transport and destroyed during a bombing. For a while the Mercury ran the overnight mail between South-ampton and Alexandria. Shortly after the demise of its huge partner, it was scrapped."

Brahe put his hand on the instrument panel of red Bake-lite with oval gauges and clearly outlined numerals. "But that was the beginning of the big aircraft carriers."

"True," said Epstein. "It's curious how names come back. The seaplanes built by Short were called 'empire boats,' 'impe-rial boats,' 'sky boats.' The American space shuttles returned to base hooked to the fuselage of a 'jumbo.' Perhaps what I like most about your work is that an idea or a model is never completely abandoned. Because a scientific model is never true, it is only probable. But probability commands great respect where there is no certainty. It is close to coincidence yet separate."

"Yes," said Brahe.

"In any case," Epstein went on, "the seaplanes all lived to a ripe old age, like certain animals. They rose at a time of great business competition in the intercontinental airways. People wanted a plane as spacious as possible, as fast and elegant as possible, and as inexpensive as possible. Then they became involved in the war and looked, instead, for the best place to put a dome or turret for the gunner. The old models were sold off to small private companies in the Antilles or Australia, and, as you can imagine, a big, prestigious, inexpensive seaplane was ideal there. So they were flown for another twenty years, passing from one owner to the next, until a junkyard claimed them in some corner of the world, or a storm wrecked them. Many stood idle, because no one was being trained anymore to fly them. A friend of mine bought one. As a test pilot at Sikorsky he had tuned its engine thirty years before. When he learned that it was for sale, he went and got it back."

"The same friend who worked at McDonnell Douglas?" Brahe asked.

"Pardon?"

"You once told me you went to visit a friend and saw people painting letters on an airplane. Is he the one?"

Epstein smiled, gestured. "No, that was another friend."

Tourists and young people entered the piazza, wandered around, sightseeing. As they passed, they stared at Epstein's car, which had one tire on the sidewalk. Epstein observed these people in turn, with curiosity but not pointedly, as if tactfully declining to think about them or about their lives beyond the duration of their simple passage. Or so it seemed to Brahe.

Then Gilda and Rüdiger appeared, in the direction opposite to the one expected. "There they are," said Epstein.

"We did the tour of the ramparts," Rüdiger said, shrugging. Gilda saw that Brahe was half-amused and half-displeased.

"Are we very late, Pietro?" Rüdiger asked.

"No, but you made us wait," said Brahe, moving to the back seat.

Descending to the new part of the city, Epstein drove faster, feeling gradually more comfortable because there was more space. The smooth motion, the neutrality of the architecture, the quality of the light, the proximity of the water. From time to time he looked at Brahe and Rüdiger, or at Gilda by his side, who was leaning slightly backward to follow the passage of the branches.

At the intersection at the bridge, Epstein stopped the car and got out without turning off the motor. Brahe and Rüdiger also got out. Gilda took the driver's seat and said good-bye to them. Shaking Brahe's hand, she said, "I would like to see you again, Pietro," speaking seriously, without hints, and he replied, "Okay." The car moved on and turned the corner.

It was time to take their leave of Epstein. Rüdiger clicked his heels as he had done at the beginning, and Brahe said, "Maybe next week I'll fly."

"Early in the morning?" asked Epstein.

"Yes."

"And you won't work that night?"

"I probably will, but at dawn one can't always sleep."

"Would you like to fly together?"

"Okay," said Brahe for a second time.

On Quai Général Guisan, Epstein headed for the English Garden and the lakefront, toward Bellerive. Brahe and Rüdiger watched him for a while—tall in his linen jacket, resolute in his gait—then crossed the intersection and went in the opposite direction. There was an odd gray light typical of the end of certain summer days. They walked without speaking, each absorbed in his own feelings about the day, though Rüdiger occasionally glanced at Brahe, uncertain of his friend's mood. They descended the stairs on the side of the bridge leading to the underground parking lot next to the lake. Air ducts, cement walls, a car with a coat of dust, there for who knows how long. Brahe looked for, didn't find, his blue Fiat.

"We shouldn't have left the car like that, underwater," Rüdiger joked.

"We'll shovel the fish out." Brahe smiled as he gave the stub to a young man in a uniform, an Oriental.

9

Among the things that slacken as the years go by, and which therefore one must exert effort to keep in good form, is precision, and Epstein paid particular attention to precision. Not to fastidiousness, which constricts the field of vision, or to perfection, which widens it without limits, but to precision, the kind involved in building a muscle. Perhaps he felt that precision conserved wonder and that getting old meant losing not so much curiosity as one's capacity for wonder.

His precision was not snobbish. He tolerated imprecision in others, even exaggeration, so long as they could help in the understanding of something. For him, precision was the easiest way of arriving at and preserving wonder. Fortunately, there were still things for which wonder came spontaneously, without effort. The most wonderful thing was, had always been, sleep. Not dreams, not that subterranean continuity that bound day to night—it was sleep itself that was the mystery. Abandonment of individuality. Animal brotherhood.

Regeneration. One should pity insomniacs, he thought, for they were deprived of something truly great.

Precision, now that he has risen, dressed, poured his coffee, and is standing on the veranda looking at the already formed day but waiting for the sun, precision would be—if he were still writing his stories instead of seeing them—exact expression. This type of air, this type of light, this consistency, this tension on the skin of the face. It means selecting among all adjectives the one that gives the correct degree of humidity and humor, of temperature and temperament, of cloudiness and lucidity; in brief, what fuses the perception and the feeling.

Epstein has never been able to conceive a character or a situation or a sentiment outside a particular physical context, believing that atmosphere should be exactly that, the literal mass of air that surrounds a story. Sometimes it has been enough to think of the context and not describe it, in which case even the air and the light end up in that scaffolding of a story which one detaches and discards once the story can stand on its own. His work, he realizes, is full of such cadavers: a massacre of possibilities on every page, a cemetery of objects and gestures, images and thoughts dismantled and spread out on the ground. For this reason, rereading is painful, because what one sees is only the developed picture, while the author keeps within him the memory of all the negatives. But then little by little he forgets, and as he rereads, the entire story comes to seem, as he wished, written by someone else. Good, that he has survived all this.

Now the air and light are important in a different way: no longer the backdrop but the things themselves, and figures perhaps. But to this—to the light, above all—he will give thought later. His back to the house, his shirt-sleeves rolled up, he holds his cup of coffee and thinks that for him precision would have been, once, a description of the amorphous dots that at this exact moment wander across his eyes, floating, transparent, visible only against the blue of the sky; a description of their movement, which is a little slower than the movement of the eyes and not completely controllable, like the snow in domed paperweights; a desirable description, because at this exact moment, in some part of the world, there is someone who sees them as he does, and from this external time may be measured, and the time that is within; but now he cannot see them, he begins to see, instead, a story, its air, light, objects, and characters, a story whose precision is internal, no longer dependent on him: a thing separate, as the bubble is separate from the glassblower.

After a while he went back inside, to the study, put the cup on the desk, and took from one of the drawers his pilot's license. He heard the footsteps of the gardener, who always entered the house without announcing himself, since his simple presence was honor enough. A large sun was rising, reflected on the glass wall.

As Epstein crossed a Geneva devoid of traffic, slowing almost to a stop at a blinking yellow light, he asked himself if today he should address Pietro Brahe in the familiar second-person singular. But the *tu* was irreversible, a difficult passage, a step that diminished the reserve of possibilities. Perhaps the deeper friendships were those that used the formal pronoun, which set up small boundaries. . . .

The mechanic saw them arrive together: walking along the row of lime trees, along the grass airstrip. The young, tall one was Pietro Brahe; the one with white hair had to be the owner of the Zlin, whom the mechanic would finally meet.

Now all three were in the hangar, looking at the pan into which every now and then a drop of oil fell, coming from the tarpaulin-covered Zlin.

"If you had telephoned," said the mechanic, "I could have told you."

"When did it start?" Epstein asked.

"About ten days ago. It is losing only a little, but it is losing."

"The last time I flew, the oil pressure was normal."

"The last time you flew was several months ago. Had I known you as I know all the others who keep their planes here, I would have asked you to take it up every so often. But I never saw you. And I had no authorization to take it up myself."

They discussed the damage. The mechanic put his finger under the leak, waited for a drop to form, looked at the drop, then shook it off his finger sharply, as one shakes a thermometer. "Probably a gasket," he said.

Epstein asked the mechanic to replace the engine when he had the time, if necessary, and also told him that from now on he had permission to fly the Zlin. And apologized for not having given that permission sooner.

Since they had come to fly, Brahe pointed to a white-and-blue plane on the cement pad. "Shall we take the Cessna?"

"Isn't that the one you usually take?" asked Epstein.

"Yes." Brahe nodded. He had reason to remember it.

"Let's try something else." Epstein inspected the planes in the hangar; he asked the mechanic the rental for each.

There was a brand-new Mudry Cap 10, a light, swift plane with low wings and a cockpit canopy of tinted Plexiglas. The mechanic helped them push it out of the storage area and onto the cement pad. There Epstein looked it over—more in appreciation of the workmanship than to check it, or at least giving that impression, in order not to offend the mechanic. He observed the sturdy frame, the tail, the ailerons, the landing gear. "A beauty, isn't it?" he said to Brahe, and Brahe nodded.

Epstein climbed aboard from the left, Brahe from the right. Once inside, Epstein found the instruments, dials, and switches at a glance. "As if he'd just left this plane," thought Brahe.

Without even removing his jacket, Epstein clicked the starter a few times, checked the fuel gauge, and put the engine on idle. While the oil was heating, he said, "Sure you're not too tired?"—shouting over the noise, over the wind from the propeller.

"I'm sure." And in fact it was not at the junction of night and day that Brahe got sleepy. If anything, dawn gave him energy. The only discontinuity was that things of the preceding night appeared very far away, much farther than they would the day after. He thought of Rüdiger, who had decided to stay into the next shift, after Mark's arrival, and said, as Brahe was leaving, "Say hello to Epstein for me." Brahe, fingering the instrument panel, looking for the tachometer, shouted to Epstein, "Regards from Rüdiger."

Epstein nodded, pulled down the canopy, which shut out the noise, checked the oil pressure, and increased the gas. Brahe checked the altimeter, altitude and heading indicators. Epstein opened the throttle all the way and increased the RPM. Brahe moved the stick, looked left and right to see if the ailerons raised and lowered, put his feet on the pedals and turned to see if the rudder responded. Epstein fastened his seatbelt, and Brahe fastened his. The plane moved forward. Brahe nodded to the mechanic, who nodded back, against the still-red sky.

From that moment, the air was no longer the same: it sought the propeller, it clung to the wings, fuselage, empennage, forming an immobile veil, a first stratum over which other strata flowed, curling from the resistance. Molecules of air aligned themselves into flowing veins of increasing substantiality; they shifted, created vacuums, gathered around the entire shape of the plane. At the wings they separated, passing over and under, more free to run on the top, more obstructed beneath the belly, then came against the vertical rudder, which split them left and right. The air entered the cylinders, creating a cold continuity that tempered the infernal heat of the air that with other vapors exploded inside, that pushed or pulled against valves, opening and closing them, that penetrated by pipes and plugs to the instruments and was there transformed into numbers of increasing velocity as Brahe watched. The air pushed, engulfed itself on fixed edges and fixed sides, and on movable edges and movable sides, making Epstein grasp his stick and Brahe use his pedal. The air became more and more solid, until, three-fourths down the runway, it pulled them up. It did all this while standing still, from its point of view.

They were flying level, without a cloud in the sky. Keeping an eye on the dials, calculating the wind direction, converting knots to kilometers and feet to meters. Supported by the air that pushed almost horizontally on the wing flaps, keeping the plane at the same altitude.

"Where to?" asked Epstein.

"The Caribbean," said Brahe.

"Not enough fuel." Epstein smiled. Checking the altimeter and air speed indicator, he said, "You never invited me to the place where you work. Couldn't we go there?"

"Yes, but one can't see anything from the outside."

"Doesn't matter. Since we have to circle back from somewhere, the ride at least will make sense."

Brahe looked down, tried to identify the streets. Using the mountains as a reference, he pointed to one of the smaller towns among rectangles of yellow and green: "Echenevex, at the foot of the Juras."

Epstein nodded, moved the stick to the left, and the aileron on that side lifted, and the one on the opposite side lowered, banking the plane by a few degrees. Brahe pressed the pedal lightly, helping with the rudder. He touched the throttle to compensate for the loss of power and maintain altitude, but Epstein said, "No, let's descend a little."

They made a wide turn, almost a full circle, until once again the air found the surfaces equal and stabilized the plane on the horizontal. They were low and speeding over fields, roads like raised veins, over smooth patches, blemishes, wrinkles: the skin of the landscape.

"This little plane isn't bad," said Epstein.

"Not bad at all, good balance, very responsive," said Brahe. He nudged the wheel left and right, testing the stability.

Then above Echenevex he recognized the church bell tower and the square, except that the things that one was accustomed to seeing from below were, from this height, curiously different. They moved too quickly—one could not turn back to a detail—such as the waiter standing at the café door, the café where Brahe had stopped just an hour before. The waiter was looking up at the plane passing low over the rooftops. "That way," said Brahe, pointing to a street that led out of town to the left. A moment later, they were circling slowly over the big beige-and-blue hangar with air vents, surrounded by beech trees, in the clear morning sun.

Epstein looked down attentively, saying nothing. Brahe saw Rüdiger's car still in the lot, next to Mark's black Jaguar, and felt that he was too high, too distant, too removed. During the long weeks of the experiment, this remoteness seemed to diminish his energy. Even during the free hours of the day, hours needed for sleep and relaxation, he had forced himself to stay within the experiment's tension, as if that participation would somehow help. Then he realized that the most progress was made while one was distracted, not concentrating, and thus he learned the necessity of diversion. But it had taken him time to overcome the fear that without concentration there could be no memory, and even now, up here with Epstein, he asks himself (a brief pause) if this is a moment of diversion or concentration within the mystery of their friendship.

They leave Echenevex, flying low over the plain in a slow, wide circle, following the invisible circumference of the underground ring. They pass Crozet, St. Genis, the original

Meyrin installation, Les Vernes; they skirt the international airport at Geneva, asking permission to fly over, and follow the circle above Ferney, where Brahe points out the small villa and Voltaire's Castle. They fly over Collex and Versonnex. In the air, at about seventy knots, their rotation above the ring seems stationary compared with the speed of light of the stream within it.

The hangar reappears, distant on the edge of the little towns, half-hidden in small woods of alder and maple. A laminated sky-blue roof, high walls, a few cars parked on the side. Each time they pass over and Brahe says "There!" and explains things, Epstein, with a slight tilt of the head, moves his eyes from the instruments to the vista below. He watches, but not excessively, as if he already knows, or as if this is only a point of departure.

They complete the circle within range of Echenevex. Epstein says, "Very pretty." He accelerates, and the air lifts them back to cruising altitude.

Then, flying high and in no particular direction, keeping the city, the lake, and the Rhone on the left, Epstein touches his temple and says in an offhand way, "You never told me about your experiment."

"You never asked," says Brahe, squinting from the light.

"Is it classified?"

"No." Brahe smiles. "Anyone can come to see. There are no guards, no secrets. Except that you have to give advance notice. Down there, the doors are automatic, because of radio-activity; if someone opens them without proper precautions, everything stops."

"And how do you protect yourselves?"

"From the visitors?"

"No, from the radioactivity."

"With film."

"The film you use to photograph the children?"

"No," says Brahe, smiling. He searches in his pocket for the badge and passes it to Epstein. "I have to put that on every time I'm there. Inside is film. At the end of the month, they take it out and see how much radiation I've been exposed to. The readings go from zero to four. If I don't show up with the film-badge at the end of the month, they list me as a four, which means I'm dead." But he adds, "The ring itself is shielded by concrete blocks. Anyway, in collisions between electrons and positrons the radiation level is low—not what it is with protons and antiprotons."

"Ah, good," says Epstein, returning the badge.

Then, stretching his hand to the instrument panel, he turns off the two-way radio that has been on since they passed the Geneva airport, filled with voices and crackling between the control tower and approaching pilots. He fingers the throttle, pulls it, and they climb through degrees of green and brown and gray to transparent white, beyond the peaks of the mountains.

"And so? Your experiment?" says Epstein, eyes on the horizon.

Brahe looks at him. Square-shouldered, head held slightly back, a crown of expressive wrinkles at the corner of his eyes, Epstein is smiling easily, but he is waiting.

At first Brahe seeks images, analogies; he even gestures, like an actor trying to convey a feeling. But as soon as he says "As if," to make visible what is not visible, to put into space what does not occupy space, to give form to what is formless, Epstein interrupts him:

"No, not like that. That doesn't help. What you are describing doesn't resemble other things—you know that perfectly well. I want to feel this difference. The things that will originate from your experiment will be nonthings. Why should I imagine them in terms of the things that already are, and that are disappearing? Why would you have me receive them without their names, however arbitrary their names may be? Why set up a dummy, a mirror before me, which impedes my perception of the otherness? Don't worry about confusing me, because this is completely outside my field of competence. Please, start again. Talk as though you were talking to Rüdiger, as though you were talking to yourself."

Brahe nods, "Very well," and for the first time tells Epstein everything, calling everything by its proper name, its proper sign, its proper formula. He gestures little, removing his hand from the stick more to offer his ideas than to illustrate them, as if summoning, from the underworld, dimensions, movements, states, and directions that arise mathematically and exist, resilient and astonishing, only in mathematics. To speak of up and down, of inside and out, is meaningless, and now and then Brahe has to correct himself and start again. Checking Epstein with a glance, he discovers that the more he talks to himself, the more Epstein seems to understand.

Listening, Epstein leans toward Brahe, and Brahe, speaking, leans toward Epstein, and they are so immersed in each other, and the noise around them is so continuous and enveloping, like the air, that an eavesdropper, next to them, would not be able to hear a word.

10

Through the slats of the venetian blind, a ray of light, sharp, concentrated, catches dust motes suspended in the air. The specks, though everywhere, seem to enter from shadow, move slowly through the light, then disappear ceilingward or floorward, again into shadow. Brahe watches them from his bed, at noon, half-awake. He thinks: Why can't everything be visible like this, naturally? If, from the beginning of recorded time, a standard unit of perception had not been selected and imposed, perhaps today there would be no need for his work. He thinks of that unit as common sense, the extraordinary influence, ease, and intolerance of common sense, even though it occupies a very small band on the spectrum of what one can feel.

Brahe had spent the night recalibrating the detector with Rüdiger. Mark had been there, too, since the memory was involved. They installed a new trigger threshold, eliminating one whole series of signals to focus on another. At dawn, when they went back to the surface without having seen anything, he felt the lingering suspicion that their effort was useless, that it would have been better to leave the detector as it was.

A conversation in the garden—Eileen and Sarad—rises through the window. They speak in low tones and with long intervals, like a convoy of trucks: it moves jerkily, then stops. Eileen and Sarad, in turn, know that Brahe is awake by the sounds he makes straightening up the room, putting the day in order, since one's life in a house is made up of these small signs of presence and activity. Eileen and Sarad interpret correctly, also, the fact that the telephone rings only twice before Brahe responds.

"Do you think one can visit Voltaire's Castle today?" Gilda asked.

"Perhaps. It depends on the hours. Besides, today is Sunday," said Brahe. To find a natural tone, deep breath was necessary, a more upright posture in front of the phone.

"You said it would be open in August or September, remember?"

With his finger Brahe lifted the louvers of the venetian blind. The gate was not visible from his window, but the roofs, the closed shutters on the main floors, and the empty park were. "I don't think it's open."

"But one can come and look at it from the outside. That's possible, isn't it?"

"Of course," said Brahe.

"And you would come to see it?"

"All right." Brahe, smiling, gave her directions to the villa. She set the time.

"Voltaire's Castle is that important to you?" asked Brahe gently.

There was a moment of silence, then Gilda, a smile in her voice, said, "Not that important," and hung up.

Brahe washed, shaved carefully, but hurriedly, which was inexplicable, since there was plenty of time. Before going downstairs, he glanced at himself in the mirror. Linen pants, and a white shirt turned up at the wrists.

In the garden he ate, without complaining, the rice salad prepared by Sarad, though it was full of hot peppers. He teased Eileen about the attention she paid to the knot on her shoulder that kept the upper part of her outfit from falling. He reviewed with Sarad everything that was presently known about gravitational waves. The Indian had set up the resonance cylinder and was now waiting for something from the universe.

But Brahe listened with half an ear, thinking instead about these temporary cohabitations entered into with such ease, and which left him only with an acquaintance with the English language that more and more resembled a submergence in water, and with the image of mail on small tables in the entrance halls of homes, envelopes differing widely in their handwriting and stamps but all bordered red and blue: PAR AVION. Brahe spoke, smiling, about the fact that, without being aware of it, one aged more quickly in a gravitational field than in the absence of gravity, but he was thinking about the coming afternoon and the continuity from his date with Gilda to the evening and night in the lab with Rüdiger, and, further still, to the moment when all this would be remembered, assuming he remembered it. For a moment he feared he might not, and experienced a nostalgia, a sudden nostalgia for this lost afternoon in which he spoke with an Indian superficially about gravity while his ear strained to hear the cars on the street, the scrape of the gate, the noise of the gravel drive—until he heard them, much sooner than he had expected, and got up, letting the sentence drop halfway, on the word "gravitons." He walked toward Gilda in the garden and asked, "Did you have trouble finding the place?"

"Why, no, you gave me excellent directions," said Gilda.

Brahe introduced Sarad and Eileen, and when he said "an astrophysicist," Gilda smiled at the beard of the young Indian, and when Brahe said "a builder of magnets," she looked at Eileen's shoulders, as if Eileen built them by the strength of her arms. Then Gilda drank the mint tea Sarad offered and spoke with Eileen about the amount of light (but not of sun) that certain indoor plants required. But it was obvious, in the way she addressed the other two, and in her nonchalance when she asked, "Your windows are the ones up there?" that she had come for Brahe. And, having observed the amenities, she took him in tow.

They were at the castle in no time, and, looking through the bars of the gate, Gilda saw that Brahe had been right: it wasn't a true castle with turrets and merlons, but a gray, linear, seventeenth-century edifice with a roof in four sloping planes and many dormers. On the whole, it was spiny and too self-conscious, like the fir tree whose branches had been shaped to make a perfect cone. Two stairways led to the castle, widened at the bottom like two tongues.

Neither Gilda nor Brahe minded that it was closed. But

as they turned away, back to the tree-lined avenue, a delivery van swerved up to the gate, stopped, and a young man in overalls and boots got out. He looked at them, then at the gate, and asked, "Did you want to see the castle?"

Brahe looked at Gilda, realizing that although the invitation was no longer welcome, they somehow still had to respect it. He said, "Yes," and added, "Are you the custodian?"

"Custodian?" laughed the young man in overalls, taking from the van a toolbox with a long strap, the kind that plumbers carried. "I'm the owner. The son of the owner. I'll be inheriting the place, I mean."

"Fine," Brahe said, not interested in the disposition of the property.

The young man inserted a key and opened the gate; he nodded toward the brass plate on the side, the visiting hours. "I can't always be here to open the castle for tourists. But people *should* have the opportunity to visit."

"Yes," said Gilda, raising an eyebrow. "But if people come and find no one?"

"That doesn't matter," replied the young man. "The important thing is that they have the opportunity."

"Absolutely," said Brahe, touching Gilda's elbow as they followed the footpath.

Passing the fir, they finally saw the front of the villa unobstructed: pilasters, reliefs of fake columns rising to the dormers, shuttered windows, a central staircase, and a door of light oak.

"Very nice," said Brahe, and was heading for the door, but the young man in overalls said, "You can see the park, too," putting the toolbox aside on the ground.

The park, on the sides and in the rear, was larger than they imagined, and it was the sort of park that had to be seen thoroughly, each hedge, each work of topiary, the small trees trimmed in the shape of goblets or vases, or espaliered. The young man, with his long hair and pale eyes, escorted them through with the confident air of a master gardener, saying, "And what do you think of this?" But since he addressed himself exclusively to Gilda, Brahe was free to reflect on the reason these trees were treated like sculpture and not allowed to grow naturally. Then their guide said that he had received a higher degree but returned to Ferney to cultivate his own land—or, rather, the land that one day would be his, "if those people in the ring don't blow us all sky-high," and Gilda shot a glance at Brahe, who shook his head. Brahe studied her, her sleeveless blouse, the color and texture of her skin, the shape of her shoulders, the white skirt tight around her waist, her light and linear step.

At the end of the tour, they found themselves once again facing the wooden door, in the hot afternoon sun. "And inside," said Brahe, pointing. "Can't we have a look inside?"

"Ah, inside," said the young man, but he lowered his eyes, and his voice became so different that Gilda asked with a laugh, "Can't we see it?"

"Very well." He sighed, pulled a bunch of keys out of his overalls pocket, and immediately found the right one. He opened the door but did not go in.

"Aren't you coming?" asked Brahe.

"You can manage by yourselves."

Gilda had already entered. Brahe went in and saw, both left and right, the bottom steps of the double stairs that curved up toward each other. That was all he could see in the light of the open door. He went outside again and shouted at the young man, who was already some distance into the park, "But there's no electricity!" The owner half-turned, shrugged, and continued on his way.

Brahe goes in again. Gilda is waiting for him, uncertain, at the spot just before the dark becomes complete. They decide to continue, at least to the atrium at the top of the stairs. They climb. Brahe holds Gilda's elbow with his right hand, keeping his left in contact with the wall, and dust and plaster powder collect on his fingers. Perhaps there was a turn they did not notice, but they find themselves, at the top, still in total darkness, and behind them, the direction of their return, it is also dark. They grope forward, trying to keep equidistant from the walls, in the center, so as not to bump into the furniture, and waiting for their eyes to grow accustomed to the dark and catch, perhaps, a thread of light from a distant window, but none appears. They take shorter steps as their sense of direction leaves them. If Brahe had a cane, he would not be able to tell if he was holding it before him to avoid falling onto a couch or if it was behind him, as if propping him on an incline. The darkness is not fear, it is a different relationship with space. A moment ago, one was supported by the hierarchy of the five senses, but now touch, hearing, and smell are deputized to substitute for vision, and they produce an image of an interior that, though corresponding to nothing, determines the position of the body. If a light were suddenly turned on, the body would appear strangely displaced and confused. Brahe, tired of this, lets go of Gilda's elbow and moves decisively here, there, arms outstretched and the palms of his hands open for possible collisions. He collides in fact with the wall, which was closer than he thought. He moves his hand along fabric, to wood, to glass, to a handle that turns without any problem, and a key that offers resistance. Finally a rod slides, and Brahe throws open the shutters and says, "Oh!"

He turns and sees Gilda with her mouth open, squinting from the light. They look. There is nothing on the walls, nothing on the floor, nothing in the main hall or in the other rooms visible through one open door after another. He is too uneasy to laugh, and she is too. Then, from down in the park, the young man shouts, "What are you doing? Close them! Close the shutters!"

They closed the shutters and went downstairs quickly—quickly, not because of the young man, but in order not to forget the location of the rooms and halls leading to the top of the stairs, to keep a mental image in the darkness. Taking the last steps, seeing their feet again, was a relief.

The young man was waiting for them seated on the outside steps. Dusting off his hands, Brahe asked, "And the furniture?"

"The furniture," said the young man, and he looked toward the park. "In the changes from owner to owner, little by little, everything went. Paintings, tables, sofas, bureaus. Of course, there was less and less need for furniture." He sighed. "It's because of the furniture that the windows have to be shuttered."

"But why, if there is no furniture?"

"Every piece, you see, left a print of itself on the walls.

That's why my mother doesn't want the windows opened. The light, with time, would equalize everything, removing the outlines of the paintings and mirrors, making the fabric on the walls the same everywhere."

The young man got up, closed the door, locked it, and put the key in his pocket. Then he accompanied them as far as the gate, and in the process an awareness must have stirred in him—if not of himself, at least of his future property—because during the leavetaking he looked back at the park and the castle and said, "It was good to see it again."

Walking along the tree-lined avenue, Gilda and Brahe said little. They smiled, shaking their heads. To the right and left, fields lay in a warm halo of green light. Above, the green transparency of the beech and chestnut trees. Then Gilda said, "But isn't it ironic that your ring should go under Ferney-Voltaire?"

"It isn't *my* ring," Brahe replied. "And if you mean Voltaire's home, it also passes under Jules Verne, since there's a little town called Les Vernes. And under Villeneuve."

"Villeneuve and what?" asked Gilda, smiling. "France is full of little towns called Villeneuve-and-something."

"Villeneuve, the pilot," said Brahe.

"Did you admire him?" she asked, touching her ear.

"Partly."

"How, partly?"

Brahe stopped and looked at Gilda, to see if he could enter a subject that did not generally interest women. He began: "Villeneuve often didn't complete his flights. He would leave the runway, open the engine all the way, and go like a bat out of hell. He was a man who took risks. But I admired his generosity. There's another way to fly, however, which I also admire. There are pilots who calculate exactly the amount of fuel, to arrive at their destination without running dry, pilots who avoid unnecessary risks, who in a race will lose a few seconds in order not to cross that fine edge of danger that means winning by a hair."

"And what is your strategy?"

"I don't race."

"In life," she said with a quick glance.

"I don't know. Risk and safety complement each other. When I'm being generous, I force myself to remember economy, and when I'm in the economical mode, I force myself to be generous. They're two points on the same wave. If you reduced the wavelength and increased the amplitude, upping the frequency, you'd get a continuum."

"It's odd," said Gilda, passing her eyes over the trees. "You don't look like someone who disciplines himself. There's too much of the animal about you."

"But I'm a physicist!" Brahe said.

"That doesn't mean a thing." Gilda continued walking, light and slender in her white skirt. "There are people who retain a lot of animal in them. The slant of their eyes, the way they walk, or turn, or smile, or bend their head. Perhaps it is because they follow their own path. I am not like that. I am only a woman."

"A beautiful woman," said Brahe, understanding her. After a pause, he added, "And what animal would I be?"

Gilda looked at him as if assessing. "A rapid, silent

animal," she said with a touch of disappointment that it was necessary to say it.

"A fish?" asked Brahe.

"No," she smiled. "Were you shocked by my story of the glow-fish?"

"A little."

"No, you're not a fish. There's a surgeonfish and an archerfish, but there is no physicist fish. No, you're a hunting animal, with legs. Long legs."

Brahe had been ready to meet Gilda's eyes, but sometimes her eyes went to him so suddenly and rested on him so steadily, he had to seek relief to the right: the little grains of the pavement, the cheerful grass at the edge of the road, a tractor going back and forth on a distant field. When he spoke to her, he paid little attention to the words, great attention to the imperceptible signals of position, the minute changes in the tension of the body, in the angle of the shoulders, hers and his, and to a thread of meaning which he continually—simultaneously—lost and found. As to the rest, he experienced what he always experienced in such circumstances: complicity, tenderness, a sense of responsibility regarding the limits of the game, and above all an unleashed imagination.

They left the avenue and cut across the main road of Ferney, taking the side road that led to Brahe's house. In front of the house, Brahe fell back, letting Gilda decide where next. She went straight to the Saab; opening the door, she said, "Let's go to Geneva."

At the border they slowed almost to a stop. The customs officer, hand raised, approached until he recognized Brahe in the passenger's seat. They drove under the airport runway, entering thick, slow Sunday traffic. They talked about Epstein. Gilda said, "There are people who have never seen him, who have never spoken to him, and yet the mere fact of his existence gives them a feeling of communion—a communion not with him, but with everything and everyone in the modern world."

Then they were walking in the center of town, not choosing streets but carried along by the conversation, and every time a silence developed, they stopped at a shop window, where objects on display prompted an appreciation or a rejection, or a question, whereby each revealed to the other something about himself, about herself, then they walked on, following this new topic. And so, too, with the houses, when they stopped to point out a building or one of the villas on the cozier streets, saying, "That's where I'd like to live," or "Not there." As if they were in the market. The choices grew larger, more ambitious, until Gilda said, "But what would you do with such a mansion?"

They walked among tourists in shorts, among young people dressed in black entering and leaving the bars. In one of the bars, where they sat down to have a drink, a video was on above their heads—and above the short, dyed haircuts of the young people. The video showed two women undressed and wrestling in a small circular arena; they grappled not with any malicious intent but with an impersonal, instinctive aggression of the flesh, of one flesh for another, as if they had never met before. The music thinned to war drums, pure rhythm, and now and then one of the women would be flat on the floor under the weight of the other, both trembling in an exhaustion first indignant, then appeasing. Finally, when one woman remained standing—surprisingly, the one with the smaller ankles—with her pelvis thrust forward and her fists clenched at her hips, and the music stopped, Gilda smiled and said, "It could never happen that way. No one can be so totally physical, so exclusively a body, with not the least reserve of inwardness. Except, perhaps, in special circumstances, and then only briefly."

Brahe agreed without giving the matter too much thought. He was intrigued, instead, by the natural way Gilda passed her glass from one hand to the other. Or how she looked at the lips of those around her. Or at his face, her blue eyes quickly checking one point, then another, as if to make sure there was no contradiction. It seemed to him then that Gilda could adapt to any environment, fitting in perfectly while remaining detached. But they were stared at by the others, because—but not only because—they were the only ones dressed in white.

In a second bar, where the stools were tall and glasses hung upside down like bells above the counter, they listened to an old black man in a white hat. He sat in a chair and played an electric guitar, singing without any concessions to the audience, severely, almost. His face was the face of a man who has played a part in the great scheme of things and is satisfied. Between songs, Gilda said to Brahe, "Have you ever noticed the structure of the blues? First you're given the topic: 'I'm telling you what it is.' Then it's repeated with the variation, 'But it could be more.' Then it turns around and says, 'Or, who knows, maybe less.' Then back to the beginning: 'No, it's really like this.' "

Outside, the sky was turning dark. They went to the car without speaking. Gilda put the key in the lock, looking at Brahe over the top of the car. He was watching the boats, lost in thought, or concerned, perhaps, about arriving late at Echenevex. Gilda, leaving the key in the lock, walked around the car and removed Brahe's hand from the door handle. Brahe, recalled to reality, wondered if for some reason she did not want to accompany him back. Pointing through the window, he said, "That's my seat, I get in on this side." She let go of his hand and raised herself by putting her arms around his neck, without looking at him.

It was a long and tender kiss, tender as only a kiss can be that one has waited for all afternoon and has given up hope of receiving.

II

It was never a particular day, although it usually happened toward the end of the week. Epstein would phone Brahe, not find him at home, and leave a simple hello for Eileen; or Brahe would call Epstein early in the morning— probably from the lab, given the pneumatic noises on the line—and say, "I could drop in this evening." Once there, Brahe waited, when the small talk was exhausted, for Epstein to come up with some semiofficial reason for the meeting. Some subject to discuss. A walk to take, which they might then give up in favor of a quiet drink. Or something a little different. For every friendship seeks its own natural rhythm, like breathing, and imagination and effort are needed to give it its character, like establishing a new habit. In addition there was the excuse that Bellerive was on the road to Echenevex at night, as from time to time Brahe would say on arriving. Or Epstein might not tell him that there would be other guests, curious to see his friend's reactions.

Once, entering the garden, Brahe met a chauffeur without a jacket seated in a dark Mercedes, and in the house there was a gentleman with white hair, elegant in a gray summer suit. The entire evening, this guest looked for an opportunity to put a certain question to Epstein, but at each lull in the conversation his nerve failed him. Finally he went and stood by the bookcase, resigned. He pulled out some books, ran a finger along their spine, checked their binding, then put them back in their place. He surveyed the entire wall of books, holding his hands behind his back. "What are you doing, Ed?" Epstein asked. Without turning around, the old man replied, "Counting the books here that have been published by me." When the time came to leave, they said ciao very simply. The publisher said, "I'm off to Zurich," but the briskness of his voice did not correspond to the sorrow in his eyes, as if the change in Epstein, whose hand he had just touched, compelled him to take note, for the first time, of the change in himself.

Sometimes Brahe brought Rüdiger along, and then their visits were shorter, he would leave sooner for Echenevex. But the conversation, the light on the plants, and the wholeness that came from Epstein were so different from this haste, that they comprised a dab of absolute color in the wheel of the week, a special respite in the increasingly frenetic passage from day to night as the end of the experiment drew nearer. Other times, on Brahe's arrival, Gilda would leave the study and come sit in the garden; she would listen more than talk. It was strange how whatever she said, no matter how unambiguous or neutral, it came out double—one meaning belonging to the conversation and the other meaning to her relationship with Brahe. Cryptic signals that Brahe, later, would try to decipher.

On the phone one morning, at one point Brahe said to Epstein, "Let's see the fireworks tonight."

"What fireworks?" asked Epstein.

"On the lake, right in front of your house."

"I didn't know there were going to be fireworks tonight."

"You weren't supposed to know. It's a surprise, a little homage to you from the citizens of Geneva."

"You must be on the organizing committee."

"I was a consultant," said Brahe.

Epstein smiled. "Are you sure they'll be right here, in front of the house?"

"They're usually on the lake," Brahe said. "From your house you should see them very well."

"So shall I wait for you here at dinner time?" asked Epstein.

That evening, waiting for him, Epstein thought again of the fireworks initiative and found it totally out of character with Geneva's sobriety. Yet in Brahe's call there had been a seriousness, or at least so it seemed to Epstein. As he was setting up the chairs and table in the garden on the lake side, he saw a motorboat glide slowly to shore, sternforemost. It anchored facing the city and turned off all its lights but the ones on the prow.

When Brahe arrived around eight o'clock, they talked about other things, such as waking up early in the morning or going completely without sleep, but Epstein noticed that from time to time Brahe leaned to the side to see something. When finally he asked him what he was looking for, Brahe said, "Could I check the view on the lake?" They walked around the house, using the tile paths as much as they could, then went straight through the magnolias and calycanthus down to the fence, where Brahe pointed to the flat-bottomed boat still in the middle of the harbor, with flashing yellow lights. "They'll be shot from there. Fortunately we have a full view of the pontoon also."

"Isn't it enough just to see the fireworks?" asked Epstein.

"Of course, you merely lift your eyes to the sky. But it's better this way. We can see exactly where they start, and how they rise."

It was not completely dark yet, that dark in which the eyes reach their maximum receptivity. The sky was a thick blue graduated into lighter blues directly above the luminous strip of the city, the quays, the lake, and the bobbing silhouettes of the boats. The color rapidly deepened, extending the range of the lights in the garden, which were similar to streetlamps, but small, like bonsai.

On the pontoon, thin shapes reflected the yellow flashes; they seemed motionless, and it was difficult to tell whether they were people or the mortars for the fireworks. "Do you think that the men are there, too?" asked Brahe.

"I doubt it," said Epstein. "The light will be too strong, the heat too great. They must be on a small barge nearby, with remote-control detonators." He turned to Brahe with a smile and said, "While they're finishing the job, can I offer you some wine?"

Brahe, leaving the fence, smiled too and said, "Yes, thanks."

They went to the little table where Epstein had set out napkins and glasses, and where he now opened a bottle of chilled white wine. An Italian wine. Brahe thought: real friendship has a delicacy in the most mundane things; its attentions are implicit, unspoken. It finds outlets where it can, in small kindnesses that little by little become habit. And once more Brahe was struck by the neat, natural way Epstein removed the plastic around the bottle's neck, held the bottle, and turned the corkscrew, not leaning on the glass tabletop, as if his hands, each producing an equal and opposite torque, were canceling the weight of the bottle by suspending it in space. Brahe told him, "Since my first visit here, I've been struck by the way you touch objects."

Epstein pulled out the cork, poured the wine into the glass, and handed the glass to Brahe. For himself he opened a thin-necked bottle of beer. He drank directly from it, but with an unaffected grace that had nothing plebeian about it. Then he said, "At a certain age, men become nervous with their hands. Losing control, they lose patience. I've always thought that when I become like that, it's time for me to go. However, I thought the same thing about white hair. One gets used to it." After another swallow of beer, he dried his lips with a napkin and continued. "Until a few years ago I hadn't one gray hair. People thought I was dyeing it. Ridiculous. Fortunately I turned white in just one year, without passing through gray. All white. The funny thing is, that was a happy year for me, or at any rate no less happy than the others. Until then, I had considered myself genetically privileged, since my father, when he died at eighty, had only a touch of gray at the temples." Epstein smiled, tall in his white shirt. "But my father was a geographer, and geography is good for the hair."

Now there was a stirring among the boats in the harbor. Car headlights lined the big bridge and the quays like a luminous liquid still flowing slowly at its center but motionless at the edges.

"Let's have something to eat," said Epstein.

"Can I help?" asked Brahe.

"No need. Keep your seat. I'll be right back."

He returned with a large tray, one hand underneath and the other on top to hold the napkins down. But the breeze took a napkin, and Brahe went and retrieved it. Epstein put the tray on the table, removed the napkins, and surveyed, hand on hip, the sandwiches arranged in small turrets. "It's the best I could get from the chef before he left this afternoon. But if you prefer something warm, we can inspect the kitchen."

"This'll do fine."

They sat in the wicker armchairs, looking up at the dark sky, the stage for the coming performance. Discreetly Epstein checked what was in the sandwiches, rejecting those with butter, choosing the thinnest. Brahe looked at the harbor, then at his watch, then again at the harbor.

"You have to be back soon at Echenevex?" asked Epstein.

"No. I told Rüdiger I'd be a little late and that he should start without me. Maybe I'll give him a call later."

"So you're not indispensable," said Epstein.

"I'm afraid I am," laughed Brahe. "But Rüdiger can manage without me at the beginning. In this stage we're never alone, anyway. Someone always stays beyond his shift or shows up when he's not scheduled. No one wants to leave, everyone wants to be present."

"It's a special stage?"

"These are the final weeks, and the probabilities increase," Brahe said. He added, smiling slightly, "The probability, too, of seeing nothing."

"I understand."

They fell silent, noticing that the windows of the top floor of each building across the lake were lighted. People working overtime? No, it is probably that these are the best observation points. Brahe brushed his eyebrow, a sign, Epstein knew, of tension. Not because of the experiment: Brahe was anxious about the fireworks—as if, though the spectacle was public, he were personally responsible for its success. He looked around and said, "Perhaps it would be better to turn these lights off."

"Like a pilot who darkens his cabin to maximize the visibility outside?"

With a smile Epstein rose, went to the house, and turned off the garden lights. A moment later he was back in the chair, resting his cheek on his hand. Brahe looked up at the sky and was about to say, "Isn't it better like this?" when two loud bangs shook the lake, the signal that the fireworks were beginning. There was a sudden hush among the boats by the shore, and the noise of the city ceased. From the pontoon, three small yellow snakes flew upward like spermatozoa impregnating the sky with the first flush of light.

The fireworks lasted a long time, so long that at the end both Epstein and Brahe felt pain in the back of their necks.

At the beginning, in the dark pauses between the first dazzling spurts, they leaned toward each other in their wicker chairs and exchanged short, quick words to express an excitement, a childish excitement, for children love fireworks. Then, as time passed, they spoke less, settling into a receptive, inward silence, each absorbed in what he saw, the loss of proportion, perspective, measurement, of up and down, right and left, the rumbling counterpoint of emotion, sound, and sight, the sheets of color that uncovered the dark, and the oohs and aahs that came from the boats along the shore.

Sometimes Epstein's profile was included in Brahe's frame of vision. The chin resting on the hand. The body either leaning forward or relaxed against the back of the chair. The concentration of the face. At one point Epstein became aware, with a start, that he was being observed, and after that kept his eyes steadily on the sky, without looking at Brahe, until the last fireworks, the strongest explosions of light, were replaced by darkness and a silence so thick, it seemed like noise. Then the cars on the bridge and shore and the sirens of the larger boats all hooted together. From one of the boats a flare shot into the sky: as if to the statement of light the best reply was more light.

Epstein and Brahe were silent. If one has the time, there are things whose activity one can follow, like the boats that now start their engines and weigh anchor, or the windows that wink out one after another in the buildings across the lake, or the people on the grass and sand behind the fence, whose arrival went unnoticed during the fireworks. But this silence between Epstein and Brahe was curious. And the way Brahe stared into the dark, not looking at Epstein, who cast a furtive glance at him, then contemplated the outline of the plants in the garden, or the bottle in his hand.

Then Brahe said, "I should call Rüdiger."

"Of course."

Epstein accompanied him into the house and turned the lights on in the study. As he went back out, he pressed the switch that turned on the lights in the garden, too. Brahe, putting his hand over the receiver, called, "Could we leave the lights off?" Explaining, "After so much light, it's more relaxing."

"As you wish," said Epstein, smiling but a little puzzled.

Returning to the garden, he decided to walk down to the fence. He strolled, arms folded, parallel to the vapor that now slid over the surface of the water, for this, though one of the last, was a summer night. Then it occurred to him that Brahe would want him to stay seated. He went to the table, took a sandwich from the tray, first touching its inside edge with his finger, since in the darkness he was unsure of its content. He ate standing, thinking that Brahe's phone conversation was unusually long.

"Any news?" he asked, hearing Brahe return.

"I don't think so," Brahe said. "You can never tell with Rüdiger, but I have the impression that there's nothing new."

Epstein touched the tray, said, "Have some more," and poured more wine into his glass. Then he sat, and Brahe sat, moving his chair next to Epstein's.

They looked at the harbor. Brahe said, "The fireworks were beautiful, weren't they?"

"Indeed," said Epstein guardedly.

"You didn't like them?"

"Since they were a tribute to me, how can I not have liked them?" said Epstein, smiling. But added, "However, as regards light, I was expecting something more up-to-date from a physicist in high energy."

"How up-to-date?" Brahe was amused at the idea that there could be progress in entertainment.

"Well, something more recent than a thirteenth-century Chinese invention."

"This is what Geneva has to offer in the summer," said Brahe, stretching out his hand in the dark toward the city.

"I know. But it was you who asked me to see the fireworks. I watched them carefully. Energy is not my field, but I assume that from the point of view of physics great progress has been made there since the thirteenth century." He also took a sandwich, then said, smiling, "Or, perhaps, in some ways, there has been no progress."

Brahe grew pensive. "Symmetry," he said slowly.

Epstein took a bite from his sandwich. Then he said, "Symmetry is that thing according to which," and he switched unexpectedly into Italian, *S'ode a destra uno squillo di tromba, a sinistra risponde uno squillo?"* The vowels were a little slurred, but it was good Italian.

Brahe was momentarily taken aback by this incursion into his native language and because of the famous line. Then he smiled. "Yes, true. The symmetry I use is a bit more

---

*"One hears, from the right, a blare of trumpets, and, on the left, another blare responds." From Alessandro Manzoni's *Il conte di Carmagnola* (Act II, Scene 6). The situation: a signaling between armies.—TRANS.

complicated, but the principle is the same, dating back to things much older than fireworks. Many scientists' enthusiasm is entirely for machines, big or little, but I'm concerned mainly with geometry. With symmetry—a very advanced symmetry. It's always surprising that through symmetry one is able to deduce other things, other dynamics. But yes, light too is symmetrical, and what you saw a while ago in the sky is not that different from what I observe under the ground in Echenevex." After a pause, he added, "But I've shown you where I work, I've told you what I see—as well as what perhaps I'll never see. And you haven't shown me what you see, or invited me to the place of its production."

"So, that's what's bothering you."

Epstein, smiling, turned to Brahe, but in the dark saw only his white shirt between the lapels of his summer jacket, the profile of his nose, his eyebrows. He looked again at the lake, and said, "Yes, I would like to share my work with you, as you have yours with me, and show you the place of its production, as you showed me the thirty-kilometer ring. But how am I to invite you to visit a verb tense, or a conjunction that joins sentences in such a way that they can coexist in peace? Or show you the precise location where an image is born, a gesture, the logic of a story? Or explain the difference between the plot and what makes it? I might tell you that a story is made of episodes, an episode of sentences, a sentence of words, a word of letters. But is the letter the irreducible literary atom? No, behind the letter lies an energy, a tension that is no longer form or feeling. What is the cement that connects the feeling to the word that makes it visible, and what power is needed to liberate it, so that we can understand the mystery by which letters arrange themselves in one way and not another, enabling me to say, 'I like you,' and the miracle by which this saying corresponds to something?"

Epstein paused, looking at the yellow and white lights of the city. "It's strange for me to speak to you about this. Strange, because I was a writer, after all, of adventure stories. And then got out of it. As one gets out of a line when he reaches the beginning of it."

"I know that," Brahe said. "But you still haven't told me what you see."

Little sounds—from the chairs, from the garden—the sounds produced even by the crossing and uncrossing of legs, of breathing. Each man, in the dark, perceived by the sounds the waiting of the other. Epstein finally said, "What I see. The situation?"

"Whatever you like. The fireworks this evening."

"I don't suppose there's a prize," Epstein said, a faint smile on his lips.

"Unfortunately, no," said Brahe gently, with an instantaneous nostalgia for what he was remembering, for what he could already remember, a real past. And he raised his face to the night sky where the fireworks had been, eased back in his chair, stretched his legs, feet in the gravel.

Waiting. Nothing from Epstein. Silence, a sigh, another silence. Until Epstein began to speak in a tranquil tone. "There were two sharp blasts, without illumination, and then the display began."

"Yes," Brahe said.

"Lines," Epstein continued, ignoring the interruption, "from below entered the dark square, exploded high with a perforating boom, split where matter became light, sodium making yellow light, barium green light, copper blue light, magnesium white, strontium crimson, and calomel . . . do you know calomel?"

Brahe shook his head no, but it didn't matter.

". . . and calomel sky-blue. Lines of light branched concentrically, dropping, dimming into fires weak enough to capture the eyes without offending them, taking them on their various progressions. Immediately afterward, without either of the two spectators having the time to turn and make further remarks of appreciation, other charges sent skyward bundles of white lances that gave birth to blue lances that gave birth to green lances, fulminating rapidly for which fulmination the nitrates and chlorates, probably, provided the oxygen, transforming the air into light. . . ."

Epstein spoke with a steady breath, with no particular intonation or emphasis, only a short phrasing that set off clusters of words: "And there were slower fires, more lasting thanks to the charcoal of willows and poplars which the pyrotechnist cuts in the spring, when the sap's flow dissolves the mineral salts. Or thanks to the addition of gum arabic from acacias, which trees in this way create light, a justification of the fires that destroy, fires that are flowers with long red stamens jutting from umbrella-shaped blossoms, like the eucalyptus. Flowers with radial petals burning down into a crown of stars that go from blue to purple to white, like the passionflower. Flowers with elongated calyxes that burst into double and triple crowns of violet, like the granadilla. Flowers with a vast eiderdown of tousled stamens at the center of golden yellow corollas, like the hypericum. Flowers exploding-unfolding into filament petals of white, red, pink, and violet, like the opium poppy. Flowers launched into the sky as thick violet corn cockles that in turn effloresce endlessly, like buddleias. And flowers with only two colors, simple blooms, where potent sporophylls branch before the waiting carpels, and flowers which from their zenith plunge in long wind-sock pedicels, violet, like fuchsia, concluding part one of the fireworks. . . .

"Meanwhile," Epstein went on with a sigh, "not only flowers but animals, too, have turned to light, because of that Indian insect (I don't recall its name) which secretes from its mouth a shellac that is essential for the explosive mixture. In the intermission, then, lower fires, thin and waving, like the antennae of creatures that inhabit the ocean floor, echinoderms with violet stingers, and fans—flabella—and blinding white wire tentacles of *Protule tabulariae* or *Policheti sedentari*. Probably you can't picture *Policheti sedentari*: a golden yellow glowing crown of cilia, pulsing membranes. The explosions whiz, hiss, snarl like rabid beasts. . . .

"And iron turns to light," said Epstein, his chin cupped in his hand, "in high, continuous jets from the pontoon's mortars, to be crowned with lion manes of filings, needles, metal dust that changes into columns of orange in midsky, so bright that in the garden below, the older man averts his eyes and the younger man stares, dazzled. Jets of light crisscross, piercing the darkness above the pontoon, which is a thin black line that cuts the image in two, pulling light from below the water and sending it upward in wild fountains, as if the pontoon had pumps and not mortars, as if the very lake, turned to light, were passing up through it. . . .

135

"Then, a pause made of darkness and the expectation of the two men, for something new to burst in the heavens, but the light comes from below, instead, at lake level, where two vessels blaze up, two square-riggers complete with sails and masts, their quarterdecks made of Roman candles and Bengal lights. Slowly they move toward one another, in cascades of fire that gradually consumes the ropes and timbers. Then gear wheels spin along cables taut over the water, paddle wheels pushed by shooting nozzles, and in a slow combustion they, too, turn to light. When that is over, a globe appears, a northern hemisphere, with incandescent continents, and on each continent a temple, one of white torches, magnesium, the other in red cupolas, and from one to the other, back and forth, rockets, petards, and firecrackers travel in short parabolas, adorning each temple with multicolored flame. The two men find it amusing that Geneva, city of peace, should portray war, but the war turns to a war of light. . . .

"Then the final act of the fire begins, a salvo of grenades, a greater diapason, more dimensioned, more intense and sonorous. Little snake grenades trace luminous ellipses in the dark, pulsing grenades stripe the sky with lines parallel and converging and diverging, a thundershower of grenades spits an infinity of bright spots and independent trajectories, parachute grenades descend in slow-motion arcs and disappear, catherine wheel grenades, burning, make bright vortices, curves, spirals in space, all symmetrical, pure forms. Whole swaths of light and dark bend according to other geometries, more complex geometries, non-euclidean, including time in their equation, and spheres explode in sequence, enormous, mighty yellow stars give birth to green stars, which give birth to violet, red, the red of receding galaxies, receding to infinity if the universe is unbounded, and small blue stars, the blue shift in the spectrum of returning galaxies if the universe is bounded and they are ricocheting back from the outer limits. Each star, dying, gives birth to another, because of the fuses that link grenade to grenade like an umbilical cord, and each birth is rapid and downward, as if wanting to reach the city, the lake, the boats, and the pontoon, near which, in acrid light, tiny men are seen running to their posts, while the two spectators in the garden lean forward in their armchairs, faces raised. . . .

"The coda, then. Fireworks so constant that there is not a moment of darkness. The spheres, dying, remain in the eyes, and the eyes, when shut, reproduce them in complementary colors, green for red, orange for blue, yellow for purple, since the eye is the guardian of the spectrum. The pyrotechnists, knowing this, alternate the colors in an increasingly infernal rhythm of image and afterimage, red, yellow, purple-blue, until there is only color, color, color, the essence volatile, like camphor that makes fireworks brighter, mothballs vaporizing in closets at the end of summer, and the colors intensify, the fire blazes brighter, the thunder punctuates blue purple orange green white even white, white which you never think of as a color but as light itself, light and light and light and— darkness."

The silence in the garden was so great that it was a while before Epstein and Brahe began to hear the crickets, whose music seemed to come from the house, behind them, perhaps because sounds, like smells, collect in corners.

Then Brahe cleared his throat and said, "They were beautiful fireworks."

"May I turn on the outside lights now?" asked Epstein. "Yes, of course."

Alone, while gradually the light gives shape to the plants in the garden, Brahe tries to fix in his mind what he has just seen. To preserve it in its first clarity. If only it could have substance, solidity, be a thing to touch. He would like to touch each image, one by one, but they, instead, are fluid, continually changing, giving him the feeling of immersion, in which it is difficult to establish any fixed point of reference. Like trying to move one's ears.

When Epstein returned, they both went down to the grassy area reserved for Epstein's walks, and walked with their hands in their pockets, looking now to the lake, now to the garden, not speaking. There was no urgency to come up with a new topic of conversation. Until Epstein said, "Do you remember the first time you came here? But of course you remember."

"I remember that we spoke about time." Brahe smiled, as if he remembered only that. "You said that time could go in both directions, and I said that that was true but only below a certain threshold of size and probability. There's a line of demarcation that crosses all things, and that line is time, memory. And you said that objects were disappearing. I've tried to understand what you meant by that. A table has its own laws, laws that govern how it stands and how one sits at it, and these laws today are still valid. But—how should I put it?—the components of which the table is made, below a certain size, obey laws totally different from those obeyed by the table itself. The objects that will be made in the future—that are already here—will be made from those components." Brahe turned and looked at Epstein, smiling. "But you already know this. What I wanted to say is that the true threshold, the true dividing line is memory."

"It's for that reason, perhaps, that I returned to Europe," said Epstein, and after a second added, "In America you have the feeling that there is no spot on earth more advanced, and you understand why they went to the moon. There was no other place to go. But gradually you begin to feel that to be advanced is not enough. That one can advance by stepping backward, also, or that perhaps backward is the only real forward, provided a man has legs long enough to take that step."

Hands in his pockets, he stopped to look at the wisps of vapor fraying at the water's edge, vanishing. He went on: "I've been told that, in your field, your research team is number one."

"Yes, apparently," said Brahe. "But this is not the Olympics." Then he smiled. "We've been working on this a long time."

"The first time you came here," said Epstein, resuming his walk, "I thought you were one of the last metaphysicians, a metaphysician out to capture transcendence with a camera. Later I realized that you were not that kind of person. And yet, in certain respects, you're a very ancient person."

Talking, without noticing it, they went beyond the area reserved for walking, through the garden, past the house, to the garage, stopping from time to time, whether because Epstein, although he did not wish to detain Brahe, had more to say to him, or because Brahe, although he had to leave for Echenevex, wanted to stay. Eventually, however, they reached Brahe's car.

Epstein turned, taking in the house, garden, lake, and bright, silent city. As if resuming the thread of his idea, he said, "But it is so difficult to describe light! The word is always too large. It provides no purchase. One says 'light,' and immediately there is conjured up a phenomenon beyond measure, beyond time, everywhere in space, not circumscribed, not palpable. Whereas I would like to describe light as if it were an object—for all objects will eventually be light." He moved the gravel with one of his shoes. "One needs so many adjectives for light. With objects, it was different. An object could be described according to its function, its consistency, by what it resembled, by the things that created it, or by the great number of things *it* created in the hands of its wielders. I might say: pale light, afternoon light, cold light, waning light. But the light remains the same, only the feelings change. And then, no matter what kind of light I would mention, you would think of a different light. Strange. Light is the most common thing in the world, much more than wood or metal, and yet it is the most private, as though each of us possessed his own." Epstein took a deep breath. "Perhaps the age of objects corresponded to the age of facts. Objects and facts got along together, like dogs and children. And someone like me, if asked, 'You're writing about . . . ?', could have replied, 'Facts, only facts, pure facts. . . .' "

Brahe listened, arms folded, the heel of his shoe on the back fender. He said, "There will be new facts, different from the ones we had before."

"Precisely." Epstein smiled. "And perhaps they will have less motion, less action. Facts occupying less external space. . . ." Then, with a sigh, passing his hand through his white hair, he said, "I'm going to write an *Anatomy of Light*. It will be, perhaps, my last book."

Brahe stared, surprised.

Epstein shook his head. "I'll write it only for myself, a little book to carry with me, in my pocket. To be used as ornithologists use field guides or geographers maps. Geography, I sometimes think, is the most fundamental science, linked as it is, by its name, to the earth. And to people, because of direction and orientation. . . . Perhaps the real center of emotions is in the inner ear, the organ of balance. . . .

"Who knows," he added. "Perhaps, in the end, I'll learn a different geography, where a man, raising his eyes from the map in his hand, beholds around him a map that covers the surface of the world, but on which he is nevertheless able to put his finger at any point and say, 'I am here.' "

A silence. Again, the crickets.

Then Epstein said, in a different voice, "Apropos of geography, I wanted to tell you that in a few days I'm leaving for Germany."

Brahe stiffened, moved away from the car. "I'm sorry to hear that."

"But I'll be back to visit you." Epstein touched his friend's shoulder and added, "After all, you're not that far away."

12

"Do you want a printout or pictures in microfiche?" asks the man in the computer room.

"A printout, so I can see them immediately," says Brahe.

He is in the data center, a long, low building at the heart of the complex. On the surface, at the south edge of the ring. Always impressive, to see hundreds of meters of paper, filled with data, emerge in less than a minute from the printer. Already folded, like Chinese paper dragons. There isn't time even to look around the room, or beyond the glass, at the logic units enclosed in office cabinets of simple, neutral metal. And for each row of cabinets, a keyboard, and for each row of keyboards, a shelf of diskettes. There are two men silently at work, only two, in an enormous area, in mixed neon and afternoon light. An early October afternoon. As the paper emerges from the printer, Brahe looks at the display, the digits, and recalls a time that was already telescoping, though not as telescoped as it is now. He is not surprised by the speed with which the paper fills with data. What surprises him is that the data recorded at dawn in Echenevex are already processed by the center. Mark must have arranged this, setting up a direct line to the main computer, placing a block of memory at their disposal, with priority channels, like a length of basting thread that one puts in to pull out later. If Mark resorted to a trick of this kind, there must be a good reason.

Brahe begins reading the printout as he leaves, stopping every few steps. In this way, slowly, he reaches his car, which is parked out in front. He lays the printout on the hood, opening it like an accordion, holding it down with an elbow. He's looking for certain numbers, important numbers. Some he finds. Paths, quantities, values. Unfolding the pages like a calendar, he goes forward then back, every now and then raising his eyes to the Jura mountains, so close, or to the flags and pennants over the entrance to the installation, but sees neither mountains nor flags, only subatomic events, ordinary and extraordinary, and weighs probabilities, and controls, finally, a mounting emotion.

Refolding the printout, he jumps into the car. He takes side roads, the shortest route through the French countryside, to arrive as soon as possible in Brétigny, pick up Rüdiger, who is waiting for him at the hotel at the center of the ring, and then both go to Echenevex. Fields, villages, farmhouses pass in gray, tidy light. One of the first overcast evenings of autumn. Not a sunset, a decline nightward, the last night of the experiment.

In the hotel Brahe looks for Rüdiger at the reception desk, where they are to meet, but the receptionist shrugs, shakes her head. Brahe looks in the cafeteria. The other physicists, who say, "He was here earlier," seeing Brahe's strained smile, suddenly are full of urgent questions about Echenevex. Brahe looks in the first-floor drawing rooms with leather armchairs arranged in circles for conversation, in the glass greenhouse and the bubble-shaped room, and in the library, where two men, heads resting on their hands, are reading international bulletins, reports on the latest research. Brahe goes upstairs, ignoring the photographs hung on the reinforced concrete pillars above the greenhouse, photographs twenty years old, in which physicists with short hair and black-framed glasses and three-buttoned jackets stand with their arms folded or their hands on machines that now are history. After this row of museum pieces, he comes to the glass terrace, as though making a tour of the bridge of a ship, and there he passes old physicists with sweaters and long gray hair—some of whom are in the famous photographs along the stairs. But still no Rüdiger.

Brahe descends the stairs, worried by the light dimming in the panes of the hotel. On the second floor he turns right and goes by the soundproof doors of the auditorium without stopping. Then, after two or three steps, turns back, looks through a porthole, enters.

Halfway down the sloping rows of empty seats, Rüdiger's square shoulders. At the bottom, on the stage, a red-haired woman playing a grand piano. Behind her, a blackboard on which there are calculations, not totally erased, from the last lecture.

Brahe tiptoes down to the row behind Rüdiger—his nape and blond hair—and sits without making any noise. For a moment he is caught up in the music that echoes in the empty hall. Then he leans over and whispers, "Weren't you supposed to meet me?"

Rüdiger starts, smiles. "Yes, but . . . such beauty."

"She is beautiful."

"I mean the music."

They listen. The piece that the woman is playing is fast, romantic. She arches her back, thrusts her bosom forward, more to the melody than the tempo, as though emphasizing certain, special notes with her body.

"Life must have been easier, don't you think, back then?" whispers Rüdiger.

"For whom?"

"For everyone."

"I don't think so," says Brahe. "For us, at any rate, the place to be is here, the time to be is now."

"Why?"

Brahe moves closer to Rüdiger's ear: "Because we have three candidates. Serious candidates."

Rüdiger jumps up, the folding seat returns to the wood back with a thump, and the woman, in a difficult passage, is distracted by the noise and plays a wrong note.

On the road to Echenevex, Rüdiger turns on the overhead light and examines the printout. He says, "Fantastic!" Brahe turns off the light. Rüdiger turns it on again. In the windshield, the reflected face of Brahe at the steering wheel and Rüdiger bent over the printout. "I can't see with the light on," Brahe says, turning it off again. Rüdiger sits back, asks, "Are there really three candidates? Am I dreaming, Pietro?"

But Brahe is thinking about something Epstein once said

regarding the light in a cockpit. He recalls the sentence exactly, as if seeing it in print. And remembers, also, that Epstein is leaving early next morning. For a moment Brahe feels a sharp desire to be back in the garden on the night of the fireworks. At the same time, he feels that he is already at Echenevex, extended like a bridge, hands on one shore, feet on the other, and that both shores are drifting farther apart. But here is Echenevex.

They descend to the lab. This night passes like any other, it is neither longer nor shorter, though to them it seems sometimes longer, sometimes shorter, and sometimes it seems even that time does not pass at all. Curious, too, that in spite of the commonality of their words and actions, each retains a different personal memory of this night. For Mark, what is unforgettable is Brahe's coolness, when, at four in the morning, following the events that at that point are plain and unmistakable, for they are events that have never been seen before, he says, leaning on his elbows, "Yes, but can we really be sure?" and, "But there might be other explanations," and lists other explanations slowly, which compels them all to circle mentally through similarities, coincidences, and possibilities, considering them one at a time, until that circle is closed. Nor will Mark forget Rüdiger's gentle awe, when, at the moment of seeing, he says, "It's incredible, incredible," though awe hardly seems appropriate to what he has before his eyes: lines, lines that rise and fall, collide and cross, creating other, smaller lines, circles, curves. But the lines tell the story of a radically new, unexpected symmetry, of the unification of different, separate energies into one larger law, a law of simultaneous difference and identity, which alters the way they see.

What Rüdiger will always remember is the unintentional humor of certain remarks that night by Mark and Brahe, such as, "It comes out too much here," or "Take it in a little there," or "That matches perfectly," or "No, this doesn't fit," as if they were tailors or dressmakers or salesmen dealing with a particularly difficult customer. But this is not a clothing store, it is a physics lab, and more and more physicists gather, as the night goes on, to participate, to be present. Rüdiger will remember: a communal sleeplessness and astonishment, in which speech is abandoned for shared glances, smiles, and shakes of the head.

And Brahe? Brahe also retains some clear images, like stills from a film. Rüdiger kicking off and sailing, in his chair, between file cabinet and console, his broad arms outstretched and his fingers poised to push buttons. Mark turning toward him, glasses hanging at his chest, with an unfocused stare, as if the numbers now were palpable, and murmuring, "So, Pietro?" Brahe remembers the telegraphic exchanges with the control room at the beginning of the night, while he waited for the electron-positron beam to be established along all thirty kilometers of the ring—impersonal, curt messages, despite the fact that Brahe knew the people at the other end well and they had the same goal, the same hope. But, above all, Brahe will never forget the moment he passed suddenly from seeing with his eyes to seeing with his mind. The depth of more than four dimensions, ten, eleven, some so tightly bounded, so curved, so impossible to represent, that he feels the word "space" breaking, the letters splitting, curling into themselves like cylinders, cylinders with other cylinders inside, or nested spheres, but these cylinders and spheres, and strips and strings and spirals, are not images, do not exist visually, it is only mentally, mathematically, that he perceives the folding again of dimensions into themselves and inside the four known dimensions of space-time, where you have your familiar fields, waves, particles, including the particles that tonight they are seeing for the first time, and it seems to him that the nuclear force or the force of gravity could be sensed directly, like hearing or touch, but that in the evolution of perception such an organ was sacrificed, abandoned in favor of a band of size-temperature-humidity, and that what was once destined for a sense organ like the ear, tongue, fingertip, eye, or nose can now be sensed only through a gigantic prosthesis like the detector in front of them now. Ironic, that now evolution has brought them to see and deal with those dimensions and those entities, and suddenly it is clear to him that, from this, new objects will emerge, bringing with them new actions, perceptions, and feelings, just as Epstein said, and Brahe feels an admiring pity for the patience with which Epstein has striven to bring himself to this point, the point of pulling the thorn from the lion's paw, and he hopes with all his heart that Epstein did not seek him out only because of this, that it was not only because of this that they became friends. And Brahe remembers the sudden pang with which he looked at the clock, on a night when time meant nothing, but he calmed, telling himself that there was still time before his friend's departure, and remembers the moment in which he realized, with the immediacy of the touch of a hand, that time was double, its symmetry so perfect that their experiment, taking them forward, took them equally back, back to a great oneness lacking in the present, to when there was but a single force, and further back, finally to within an infinitesimal fraction of a second of the Big Bang itself, from which all sprang, when everything was still one, not many in dimension and essence. He remembers that at eight in the morning, when the flow of paper stopped, when the screens were blank, and when all the systems and equipment were turned off, shut down, the men leaned back in their chairs and looked at the huge underground hall, thinking about what had taken place. Thinking that to see means to push back a little further the threshold of the nonvisible, to reconstruct in the same blink of an eye what one disassembles. Thinking that, with such a large machine and such a refined geometry and such a complex mathematics, the real problem is how to domesticate infinity, to put it in coherent, concrete terms, like asking, "Do you feel warm?" and hearing the answer, "Yes, warm." That it is in this nearness and solidity of nature that true beauty is found. Then he remembers falling asleep.

Not a deep sleep, just for a moment, without closing his eyes completely, without even lowering his head, a brief pause of the mind, as happens often in the course of such nights. Rüdiger leans over to read what Brahe has written in the notebook, as if, despite what they have witnessed, still doubting, needing to see it written down, black on white, for the truth to be true. And Brahe remembers the amazement with which they all met again above ground, in the limpid morning light, and the drops of dew at the points of the leaves.

At this very moment Epstein is in the arcade of the

Geneva station. He has checked his luggage, has had tea in one of the cafés, but there is time remaining, so he walks, hands in his pockets, along the shops, which are bright and comfortable. He stops in front of a large window full of electric trains.

He takes out his glasses but does not put them on immediately. First, he surveys the whole scene, a model of the city. In the background, a diorama of the mountains. The lake, in plastic, at the center. Between the buildings go the rails, trains in motion, with dead ends, sidings, connections, crossings. All this is surrounded by a double ring of tracks, on which an intercity train runs, circles, with orange cars, and in the opposite direction, an old Bern-Lötschberg-Simplon train, cream and blue.

To the side, in the window, are locomotives of various gauges, each on a glass shelf, each on its own track. Epstein puts on his glasses, since the models are close, at eye level, and can see now the connecting rods between the wheels, the valves on the boilers, the cowcatchers, the brake hoses that hang between the couplings, the planks between the locomotives and the tenders, and the ceramic insulators on the pantograph current collectors above the trolleys. The models are so big, it takes two hands to hold them, as demonstrated by the owner of the shop, who reaches into the display area and lifts out a long green locomotive to show to a customer. Epstein, removing his glasses, recognizes the same locomotive on the model landscape, though much smaller; it pulls, on one of the inside tracks, several observation cars of the Mittelthurgau railroad, halting invariably to give the right-of-way to an orange TGV, aerodynamic in shape, then continuing on its circular way around the little lake. A special kind of imagination is needed, Epstein thinks, to wonder how many turns the TGV must make to complete the Paris-Geneva-Paris trip, for the model travels rapidly around the plastic lake. Or to picture passengers in the empty, lighted cars and engineers in the empty, unlighted locomotives. Models of things, then, serve to exercise the imagination, though there are some figures in the diorama, near the tiny houses, figures frozen in one gesture. A woman mailing a letter. A man washing his car. A man in overalls with a ladder and a pail. A man at a depot watching coal slide into a hopper car.

Epstein consults his watch as well as the clock at the end of the arcade. He runs his fingers through his hair, glances at the people entering the arcade, entering the shops, exiting, then turns again to the window with the trains and looks, though with less attention, at the two that are running full speed along the outside ring.

It is the same speed with which Brahe arrives at Bellerive, taking the road that leads to the villa. He stops in front of the gardener, at the gate, and gets out.

"He left about an hour ago," the gardener informs him.

"And the car?" asks Brahe, pointing to the Chevrolet that is being lifted onto a flatbed truck.

"The car goes with the other things," says the gardener, and gestures at the boxes of books that two men with logos on their shirts are loading in a van. "He's taking the train."

"Which train? When?" Brahe has his hand on the car door.

"Didn't you hear it on the radio?"

151

"On the radio they announce the trains that Epstein takes?"

"The famous prize. The radio said that an Epstein won it. It might be another Epstein, of course. But if not, we must recognize the fact that he is a great man, perhaps even a saint."

"I don't think it's the peace prize he's getting," Brahe says with a smile.

"Who knows! If they saw how he trampled the grass, they'd take it away from him immediately."

Brahe gets back into the car, with emotion.

The same emotion with which Epstein, taking a closer look at the diorama, notices that between the tracks and the mountains there is also a small airfield. He sees it from above, as he has seen it before, and the proportions, even, are right. He sees a plane ready for takeoff at one end of the field and asks himself, as he has asked himself before, if it's possible, and not too dangerous, to come down in a wide figure eight and pass low and fast over the airfield. He sees the ground flowing rapidly beneath him, then the row of trees, then the plane to the left, just off the ground and quickly landing again. He sees the Jura mountains approach and for an instant it looks as if he won't make it, but then they are beneath him. He sees the young man waiting, first in the center of the field with folded arms, then on the pad; sees him take a step forward, tall, with long circumflex eyebrows, and can guess what he is thinking. He sees Pietro Brahe in a bubble of Plexiglas against the Arctic sky; he sees a blond German in another bubble communicating with him in sign language; he sees an important Chinese physicist who stops in Geneva between flights to negotiate a matter of centimeters, first annoyed at the young man's resistance, but then—discovering the deception with the dots—pleased that the young man has the nerve to deceive an important Chinese physicist. It seems to Epstein that all these things are continuous and reach into the future. He sees Gilda in a doorway with her hands behind her back, sees Brahe fingering his eyebrow, sees them both asleep, she with her arm over her face, he with his nose touching her ear. He sees a woman who in a dark room in a castle, where she knows every inch, discovers that a window has been opened and says to her son, "I told you not to." He sees Brahe and Rüdiger, and an older man dressed in a colorful manner, surface from an underground supercollider after a crucial night, astonished to be outside. Full of what has happened, they look at one another without speaking, not wanting to break the bond that connects them. He sees a publisher in a car headed for Zurich but who, at the first motel, says to the driver, "Let's stop here," and in the room takes off his tie and lies on the made bed trying to remember, in every detail, a meeting of long ago, when a lanky young man with gray eyes, son of a German cartographer and an Englishwoman, brought him a manuscript, the first, and now there will be no more, and the publisher asks himself why and, asking himself this, slowly falls asleep. And in the low morning sun, the same sun that is outside the arcade, Epstein sees Brahe cut through Quai Gustave Ador, ignoring the stop signs, traffic lights, policemen—a ride quite unusual for Geneva. He sees him look at the clock on the dashboard, sees him keep his foot half on the brake and half on the accelerator, as in a race where a fraction of a second matters, and Brahe, leaving his car in the taxi lane, runs, tall as he is, across the grooved rubber surface of the station's floor, hurriedly reads the departure board, runs in the direction of the track, but in the arcade a glance to the side gives him the image of a man with white hair standing in front of a window, arms folded, and looking at electric trains. The man who sees all of this and sees this instant, the instant in which Brahe appears before him out of breath, in that instant stops seeing.

"I didn't think I'd make it."

"There's still a few minutes."

"I heard it on the radio."

"The radio had news about you, too, my friend."

"It's a day of news for both of us."

"Good."

"And now?"

"Now a new story should begin."

"And this one?"

"This one is finished."

"Really finished?"

"Really finished."

"Will someone write it?"

"I don't know. I don't think so. What was important was not to write it, but to have felt it."